**"I want you, Jace. I want to feel something besides fear...."**

"Did you ever want to escape?"

"Yes."

Too bad she couldn't move, just disappear, start a new life someplace.

Not possible with the state of Wyoming hunting her.

So maybe she couldn't leave her problems behind. Not forever. But if she could for a few moments...just for a little while...

She reached her hands toward him and rested her fingers on his belt buckle. She knew the move was forward. She'd never been so forward in her life. But she was tired of responding to what others had planned. She wanted to feel strong, to be in control.

# ANN VOSS PETERSON

# WYOMING MANHUNT

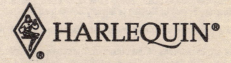

**HARLEQUIN®**

TORONTO • NEW YORK • LONDON
AMSTERDAM • PARIS • SYDNEY • HAMBURG
STOCKHOLM • ATHENS • TOKYO • MILAN • MADRID
PRAGUE • WARSAW • BUDAPEST • AUCKLAND

To Michael Voss, who wanted to live in the mountains…
so he did.

ISBN-13: 978-0-373-69316-0
ISBN-10:     0-373-69316-8

WYOMING MANHUNT

# ABOUT THE AUTHOR

Ever since she was a little girl making her own books out of construction paper, Ann Voss Peterson wanted to write. So when it came time to choose a major at the University of Wisconsin, creative writing was her only choice. Of course, writing wasn't a *practical* choice—one needs to earn a living. So Ann found various jobs, including proofreading legal transcripts, working with quarter horses and washing windows. But no matter how she earned her paycheck, she continued to write the type of stories that captured her heart and imagination—romantic suspense. Ann lives near Madison, Wisconsin, with her husband, her two young sons, her border collie and her quarter horse mare. Ann loves to hear from readers. E-mail her at ann@annvosspeterson.com or visit her Web site at annvosspeterson.com.

## Books by Ann Voss Peterson

# CAST OF CHARACTERS

*Shanna Clarke*—A hardworking accountant and single mother, Shanna believes her invitation to the Talbot Mining executive's big game-hunting trip means a promotion is on the way...until her boss starts hunting *her*.

*Jace Lantry*—A former cop scapegoated by wealth and power, Jace had given up his belief in justice, until he met Shanna. Now not only is he willing to put his life on the line to prevent her wealthy boss from getting away with murder, he finds himself wanting to open his heart...the biggest risk of all.

*Emily Clarke*—Shanna's little girl believes in heroes.

*Linda Thomas*—Shanna must rely on her best friend, Linda, to keep her daughter safe.

*Anthony Barstow*—Shanna's boss wants to kill her. The only question is why.

*Sheriff Benson Gable*—He's sworn to protect the people, but his allegiance seems to be to Barstow.

*Ron Davis*—Is Talbot Mining's chief financial officer in on the scheme, too?

*Roger Harris*—The wilderness outfitter is good at his job, but not so good at setting limits for his wealthy clients.

*Dirk Simon*—The security guard has a crush on Shanna. But how far is he willing to go to make her his?

*Boyd Davidson*—The environmental activist wants to shut down Talbot's uranium mining operation and isn't about to let anyone get in his way.

## Chapter One

Shanna felt the sound of the gunshot more than she heard it. The first sharp report jangled her nerves. The second cracked through her ear and jaw, so close she could almost feel the air stirred by the bullet. She released her mare's reins and threw her body to the ground. She hit dirt, neck snapping to the side, air exploding from her lungs. Her horse's hooves pounded the dry earth, the sound fading into the distance.

What had just happened?

Shanna raised her head. Dry brown grass swayed in front of her, sparkling with frost. White caps of mountains rose all around her. Silence hung heavy in the morning air.

Obviously someone in her hunting party had seen deer and taken a shot…and she'd let the sound scare the sense out of her.

Her cheeks heated. She'd told Mr. Barstow she was no hunter, but this would make her the laughingstock of not only her hunting party, but also all of Talbot Mining. She could hear her friend Linda's giggle now.

Shaking her head at her own ridiculousness, Shanna stifled a laugh and struggled to her feet. As long as her overreaction to the first rifle shot didn't lose her a promotion, she would laugh along. No one could say Shanna Clarke wasn't a good sport.

Brushing her gloved hands over her orange jacket and insulated pants, she peered in the direction of her fleeing horse. The mare had reached the outfitter's pack mules. The other three members of the hunting party gathered several yards away. Mr. Barstow, the CEO of Talbot, stood on the ground. Behind him, Ron Davis, the chief financial officer, and Sheriff Gable remained astride their horses. Mr. Barstow raised his rifle to his shoulder and took aim.

*At her.*

She fell back to the ground. Didn't he see her? She glanced around, expecting to see a mule deer behind her, hoping to see...

Nothing was there.

Panic slammed against her ribs. Her lungs seized, making it hard to breathe. She had to be mistaken.

She raised her head, peering over the long grass once again.

Her boss's rifle was trained on her.

She ducked before the shot cracked through the air. Her heart slammed against her ribs. Barstow was shooting at her. *Shooting at her.*

Her head swirled. It didn't make sense. None of it made sense.

She tried to rise, tried to move, but her legs were too weak to support her. She had to make them work. She had to get out of here. For her little Emily's sake. For her own sake. She didn't want to die.

Forcing herself to her hands and knees, she started to crawl, moving through the tufted, brown grass. If she remembered correctly, there was a rocky slope in this direction. Once she started down the slope, Barstow wouldn't be able to see her. She'd be able to stand without fear of being shot.

At least until he caught up.

The frozen earth was hard under her knees and hands. Her breath rasped in her throat, making it impossible to hear anything else. She imagined the sound of hooves, pounding across the valley faster than she could ever hope to move. They'd catch up to her in no time.

The ground grew rockier, digging through thick pants and gloves. She tried to move faster, waiting for the pounding hooves, waiting for the crack of gunfire, the impact of the bullet.

A report shattered the air.

Gasping, she glanced behind. Nothing but dry grass moved behind her. She forced herself to keep crawling.

The ground sloped downward. Gray rock replaced the waving grass. Shanna scrambled to her feet, forcing her legs to work. Crouching low, she stumbled over rock. Boots slipping and skidding, she picked her way down the slope. They'd be on her soon. She had to find cover. She needed a place to hide.

Another crack split the air.

She glanced behind, expecting to see horses on the edge of the slope, a rifle barrel pointed at her, but they hadn't reached her. Not yet.

The ground fell out from under her feet.

She rolled and stumbled, trying to right herself. Scrub brush scraped at her face, ripped at her coat. Jumbled sound filled her head. She landed on her hands. Pain shuddered up her arms. She pitched forward onto a shelf of rock.

Shanna gasped. Pain stabbed through her neck. She must have wrenched it. Swallowing a wave of nausea, she focused on breathing. In and out. In and out. She couldn't lie here. She couldn't wait. Barstow was coming. If he caught her…

Gritting her teeth, she rolled to her side and struggled to her knees. Her neck screamed. Her legs felt boneless. She forced herself to move, scrambling along the shelf. The rock above tongued outward, creating an overhang. She slipped underneath. Lying on her side, she curled her back into the crevice and pulled her legs in tight.

She could hear them now. The beats of hooves. Or maybe it was her imagination. It didn't matter. She couldn't check. If she peeked out from under the rock, they'd surely see her.

"Shanna?"

She tensed at the gruff sound of her boss's voice. So it wasn't her imagination. He was there. But where exactly? At the top of the ridge? Or closer? She held her breath.

"I'm sorry I scared you, Shanna. I didn't see you. I wouldn't have fired if I knew you were down range. It was an accident."

An accident? She tried to replay what had happened in her mind. The sound of the shots. The sight of Barstow lining up for shot number two. Could it have been an accident?

"Come on, Shanna. You can't think I was *trying* to shoot you."

Did she think that? Yes, she had. As soon as she saw that rifle barrel she'd thought exactly that. But did it make any sense? What possible reason could Mr. Barstow have for wanting her dead?

"You're not hurt, are you?"

He sounded worried. Shanna tightened her grip on her legs, hugging them close. She wanted it all to be a mistake. She wanted Mr. Barstow to be telling the truth, to be worried that she was hurt. But was he really? How could she have gotten everything so wrong?

"Shanna? Talk to me, honey. Tell me you're all right. Please? Shanna?"

She opened her mouth and drew in a breath. But she couldn't get the image of him raising the gun out of her head.

She closed her mouth and pressed her lips tightly together. She didn't know what to do, what to think.

"Make a sound so I know where you are. I'll get the others and we'll come down for you."

She wanted to call out. Her throat ached with it. She needed to make this nightmare go away.

The broken hiss of a whisper rode across the wind, too faint for her to catch the words.

Unease prickled all the way up her spine. It was Barstow. She was sure of it. Even in a whisper, she could recognize that commanding, gruff voice. He must be talking to someone. One of the others from the hunting party. But why whisper?

*Because he didn't want her to hear.*

She stifled the whimper struggling to break from her lips. She had no more time to think. No time to wish things were different. If she wanted to get out of this alive, if she wanted to see her little girl again, she had to move. And she had to do it now.

She tilted her head back. Pain shot through her neck. Sucking in a sharp breath, she blinked the tears from her eyes and tried to take in her surroundings. The shelf of rock stretched at least a hundred yards. If she moved carefully and quietly, maybe she could shuffle her body under the shelf. Maybe she could put some distance between her and the men without them seeing. Maybe she could get away before they found her.

She had to.

## Chapter Two

A crash sounded from up the slope. Jace Lantry glanced up from the long, clawed footprint in the patch of snow and scanned the rough terrain that rose behind his ranch. Something was running through pine and fir. Maybe the grizzly that left this footprint. Or its prey.

Tilting his hat low, he squinted at the trees, the wide brim shielding his eyes from the morning sun. He didn't have anything against the bears. Hell, the land was theirs long before humans moved in. They'd never messed with his livestock. Grizzlies rarely did. They ate plants, most of the time. But he'd better make sure the fortress he built around his garbage cans would hold. The last thing he wanted was a momma grizzly deciding his cabin would make a nice restaurant. If that happened, there was no telling what she'd assume was on the menu.

A flash of blaze orange bobbed through the clump of trees. Not bear. Hunter.

Oh, hell. When Jace had agreed to lease land to his neighbor for hunting season, he'd specified Roger could only use acreage east of Gusset Ridge. This wasn't the first time this season that a wealthy hunter had wandered past the cutoff point and gotten himself lost. Roger might be a good outfitter, but he was awful when it came to controlling his rich clients. The guy was too damn nice.

Fortunately Jace didn't have any qualms about laying down the law to a straying hunter. He'd bought this ranch in the Wyoming wilderness so he'd never have to look out for anyone but himself again. The last thing he was going to do was provide some kind of hand-holding to a wealthy SOB who didn't think he had to follow the rules.

Wait a second.

The hunter broke from the cover of Engelmann spruce and ran along the forest's edge. Shoulder-length blond hair peeked from under the orange stocking cap. The unmistakable curve of a woman's hip was evident under the boxy orange coat. She stumbled through the dry grass and occasional patch of snow, no rifle, no concern for frightening her game. In fact, *she* looked like the frightened one.

The crack of rifle fire reverberated through the trees.

The woman ducked. Slipping, she fell to her knees. Thrusting herself back to her feet, she zigged through the edge of the forest, as if certain the gunshot had been meant for her.

Something wasn't right. Not right at all. He didn't have to have been a cop in his previous life in order to figure that out. And judging from the woman's present course, she was running straight for his homestead.

Jace groaned out loud.

An eye on the woman, he headed for his cabin. He'd moved to the mountains to escape trouble. But it appeared she had found him anyway.

SHANNA CROSSED the open slope, running flat out for the small log cabin and outbuildings nestled along a stream. Her boots skidded in a patch of snow. Her breath rasped in her throat, making her ears ache almost as much as her head and neck.

Crawling under the rock shelf and the rough terrain of the slope had given her a head start against the mounted men. But that last crack of gunfire proved Barstow was still on her heels. And it wouldn't take him long to figure out where she was headed.

She had to pray she could find someone to help her, a vehicle she could borrow, or at least a place to hide.

The cabin was closest, separated from the other buildings by split-rail fencing. Shanna could only pray the place had a phone.

She reached the cabin. She sidled up to a mullioned window and peered inside. The place was rustic and simple, with the kitchen, dining area and living room all visible from the side window. She didn't see anyone inside.

She also didn't see a phone.

She closed her eyes for a moment and forced herself to take a long breath. She might be able to break in to a simple little cabin like this. But if there was no phone, that wouldn't get her very far. When she thought about it, she had no clue who to call anyway. The sheriff was with Barstow. He'd watched while her boss had lined up his shot. For all she knew, he was the one Barstow was whispering to on the ridge.

She had to get out of here, and she had to do it now.

She scanned the distance to the other buildings. A pole barn dominated the ranch, surrounded by a fence. Past the corrals and next to the barn, dirt ruts led into a square structure.

A garage?

She peeked into the cabin again, this time scanning countertops and the area around the front door for anything that looked like car keys. Nothing. But maybe that was a good sign. Maybe whoever owned this place kept his keys in the garage.

Giving the rocky slope behind the cabin a glance, she ran for the garage. She reached the first fence. She stepped over the lowest rail and ducked under the second. Sharp pain shot down her neck. She ignored it and pushed on. If Barstow caught her, a sore neck would be the least of her worries.

She ran across the corral's bare dirt, struggling to hear over her breath rasping in her throat, her heartbeat pounding in her ears. Horses looked up from the round bale they munched on. One spooked and darted through an open gate and into the larger field beyond.

Her nerves stretched taut. She tried to run faster. She had no cover. If Barstow and the others cleared the evergreens while she was still crossing to the garage, she was done for. They wouldn't have any trouble hitting her with their high-powered rifles. And she doubted Barstow would allow himself to miss this time.

She reached the other side of the fenced pen and ducked under and out. She raced to the garage. Grabbing the door-knob, she held her breath and twisted.

It turned under her hand.

She pushed the door open and slipped inside, leaving the door open a crack behind her.

The garage was dark, but with the door cracked, not too dark to see a hulking shadow parked in its center. A truck. A way out. She just had to find a key.

She strained her eyes in the dim light and groped the wall around the door, hoping to find a key hook or nail. Nothing but studs and steel. She crossed to the truck and opened the driver's door. Light shone from the cab. Fear thickening in her throat, she used the extra light to quickly scan the area for any sign of keys. Coming up empty, she climbed into the pickup's cab and closed the door.

Plunged back into darkness, she willed her eyes to adjust. She felt for a key in the ignition switch, then groped under the floor mat. Nothing. Where else might someone hide a car key? She slipped a hand between sun visor and roof.

Her fingers hit metal.

A whimper catching in her throat, she grasped the key. She tried to keep her hand steady, tried to fit key into switch.

The passenger door jerked open. Light flared all around her.

"What the hell do you think you're doing?"

Her whimper turned into a gasp as she looked into the barrel of a shotgun.

Jace waited for some kind of sound to come out of the woman's open lips. Her throat moved, but not so much as a squeak broke the silence. Hell. Looked like he'd have to help her out. "Trying to steal my truck?"

"No. I mean…" She looked down at her hand, as if just realizing she held the key. She looked back at him with a pair of the biggest green eyes he'd ever seen. "I'm sorry…I didn't… I had to… Please, don't shoot." She raised her hands in the air.

Double hell. He canted the barrel to the side. Why he should feel guilt over frightening a car thief, he didn't know. But one look at those wide eyes, those trembling lips, and the need to rush in like some sort of damn savior pulled at him like a physical force. Once a cop, always a cop, he supposed. "You can put your hands down."

She did.

"Okay, start by telling me what's going on. I don't want to shoot you. But it looks like not everyone feels the same."

She took in a shuddering breath. "My boss."

"Your boss?"

"He's trying to shoot me."

That was a new definition for the term *boss from hell.* "Why?"

She shook her head. "I don't know."

Hard to believe. It was always the same. Under interrogation, every criminal was completely innocent. Every scumbag a victim through no fault of his own. "You sure about that?"

Tears welled in her eyes. She raised her hands in front of her, as if totally at a loss. "I don't know what's going on. I swear. I thought I was up for a promotion."

Talk about not reading the signs…

Jace bit back the quip. As surreal as this whole situation seemed, it wasn't the time for jokes. If someone was gunning for this woman, he didn't want to get in front of the bullet. As a cop, he'd gone ten years without ever firing his gun. And he'd never been shot, either. He didn't plan for that to change now that he was no longer on the job.

Let the guys who *hadn't* been kicked off the force handle it. "I'll call the sheriff."

Panic streaked across her face. "No! You can't!"

He felt a tightening in his gut. He knew there was more to this. He could feel it. "Why not?"

"The sheriff. He's with them."

"He wants to kill you, too?" That was even harder to buy than the boss's sudden homicidal urge. "This keeps getting better and better."

"You've got to believe me."

He didn't *have* to do anything. "Why is the sheriff after you?"

"I don't know."

He had a guess. "You break the law?"

"No. I told you. I thought I was getting a promotion."

He let out a heavy sigh.

"I'm telling you the truth. We were supposed to be hunting deer, and my boss started shooting at me."

"And the sheriff? How does he fit in?"

"He was there. Just standing there watching."

"Are you sure it wasn't an accident? Are you sure he wasn't shooting at, say, a deer?"

Redness rimmed her eyes, as if she were about to burst into tears at any moment. "I'm sure. He came after me. He's chasing me. The others are, too."

"The others, meaning, the sheriff."

She nodded. "And the CFO of the company where I work."

This was ludicrous. He shouldn't believe her. But he'd seen her running along the line of trees. And God help him, she seemed scared out of her wits. "So what do you expect me to do? Stand out front and return fire?"

For a moment she looked at him as if that was exactly what she was thinking. She shook her head. "Of course not."

"What then?"

"Just lend me your truck. I'll return it. I promise."

He almost laughed. "You must think I'm an idiot."

She shook her head. "I know it sounds bad. But I'll return it. I swear, I will. I have to get out of here."

Movement caught his eye through the opening in the door. He held up a hand.

The woman gasped. She covered her mouth with trembling fingers.

Jace felt the weight of the shotgun. The last thing he wanted to do was get in some sort of old-west shootout. But what could he do? He might not believe everything this woman was saying, but that didn't mean he could just hand her over to people who might want to kill her and wash his hands of the whole thing. He might no longer be part of law enforcement, but he was still a cop where it counted. A true cop. At least he liked to think so.

He held out his hand, palm up. "The key."

She dropped the truck's ignition key into his hand.

"Get in the backseat and crouch down on the floor. There's a blanket back there you can use to cover yourself."

"Thank you."

He didn't know what to think about this woman. He sure didn't buy her ridiculous story. Not without some kind of evidence to back it up. And if she were lying, he'd turn her over and not even bat an eye. "Don't thank me yet."

He stuffed the truck's ignition key in his jeans pocket. Turning toward the door, he held the shotgun at the ready, took a deep breath and willed the spot running from the center of his chest to the waistband of his jeans to stop jittering.

Here went nothing.

He strode out of the garage. The brightness of the sun stunned him for a moment. Tilting his hat low over his eyes, he scanned the house, the barn, the corrals.

A heavyset man circled the fence line. Dressed in a bright orange coat and sporting a silver belly cowboy hat on his head, he held his rifle as if he intended to use it.

Jace pushed a stream of air through tight lips. It fogged in the cool autumn air. "You looking for someone?"

The man started slightly, but kept walking forward. "You the landowner?" he called out in a loud voice.

"Yes. Jason Lantry."

"I'm Benson Gable, the sheriff around here."

Jace lowered his weapon. He pulled out his best relaxed smile and plastered it to his face. "Nice to meet you, Sheriff. What can I do you for?"

The sheriff also lowered his gun and came to a stop two

yards from Jace. "There's a fugitive in the area. Looks like she was headed to your ranch here."

"She?"

He gave a sharp nod. "Reddish blond hair. She's dressed in hunting garb. Orange coat, orange hat."

"Like you."

"Yes."

Jace had been hoping the sheriff would divulge a little more. Like something that proved the woman was lying. Something that would allow Jace to turn her in and walk away with a clear conscience. Well, if the sheriff wasn't going to come out with it, there was nothing wrong with asking. "What did she do?"

"Can't go in to that. But she's armed. And definitely dangerous. Mind if I take a look around?"

"I'd like to help you, Sheriff. I really would. But there's been no woman around this place for longer than I care to think about, and I have an appointment I really have to get to." He glanced at his watch for emphasis.

"You won't mind then if we look to make sure. She might have slipped in when you weren't looking."

"We?"

"I have a deputy circling the property."

The woman's boss? The chief financial officer? Or actual deputies? With his luck, one had already slipped into the garage, found the woman, and they were about to arrest him for being an accessory to whatever crime she'd committed. He'd land back in jail without even knowing what hit him.

He stifled the shudder that thought inspired. "Got a warrant?"

The sheriff shook his massive head. "Nah. Don't worry about that."

"I'd feel better if you tell me what she's wanted for."

The sheriff hitched up his pants. "Lover's spat. Shot her boyfriend."

Was it possible? Had the woman's terror been about being caught? Had she been feeding him a line of bull?

Jace didn't know. He couldn't shake the sight of her hitting the ground at the sound of the rifle shot. No sheriff he knew would take potshots at a fleeing suspect with a deer rifle. Not if he was on the up-and-up. "I'd feel better if you had a warrant."

"No need for a warrant, son. We don't suspect you of doing anything wrong."

"Happy to hear that."

He took a step forward. Looking past Jace, he eyed the garage.

"But you'll still need a warrant."

"What's your game, son?"

"No game. I just want to protect myself. I was on the job once. Had to have a warrant for every damn thing. I figure now that I'm on this end, there might be something to it."

The sheriff gave him a look that suggested he'd rather shoot him than show him a warrant. "Where you from?"

Meaning, where had he served as a cop. "Denver."

"Figures. Things aren't done that way around here. People trust the law." He narrowed his eyes and scanned the corrals and cabin beyond. "Unless you got something to hide. You got something to hide, Jason Lantry?"

Jace held up his hands, praying he wasn't getting himself in so deep he couldn't dig himself out. "Nothing to hide. If this woman did what you say, I'll be glad to truss her up and hand her over."

Again, the sheriff eyed the garage. "What's in there?"

"My truck."

"That where you came from just now?"

Jace nodded. "Like I said, I was getting ready to head out. I have an appointment."

The sheriff's cheeks puffed into a smile. "You want me to get a warrant? You know how it works. You're going to have to stay here and wait. No way you'll make your appointment."

Jace canted his head to the side, as if considering this. It was the perfect way out. If he wanted to take it. If he trusted the woman. If he wanted to stretch his neck between the guillotine blades.

Jace tried to keep his breathing even. He'd interrogated enough bad guys to know how good lying was done. But even after all his disappointments with the Denver P.D., the idea of not cooperating with the sheriff sat in his gut like a cold stone. A cop didn't obstruct an investigation. Especially not when the most compelling reason he had to believe the suspect was a set of pretty green eyes. "Okay. Can't say I see any harm in letting you look around."

The sheriff gave a satisfied nod. He glanced in the direction of Jace's cabin. "Back door is open. I suppose it's possible she could have slipped in there."

Jace followed his gaze just in time to see a man wearing hunting gear duck around the cabin's corner.

A man whose face he recognized.

Jace glanced back at the sheriff. "One of your deputies?"

The sheriff gave him a look as if to say, it's none of your damn business. "Yup."

Jace nodded. There was no hope for an easy way out of this now. He'd seen that man on the nightly news, and he was no sheriff's deputy. He was CEO of Wyoming's most successful state-based mining operation, Anthony Barstow…and quite possibly the woman's boss.

He raised a hand and waved to the sheriff. "Okay, then. I'm

out of here. Good luck finding her." His voice sounded strained, gruff, and he could only hope the sheriff didn't notice.

He didn't seem to. Probably too busy with his own plans to make his rich friend happy by hunting down a woman with strawberry-blond hair and big green eyes. The sheriff raised a hand in a quick wave goodbye and trudged to the cabin.

Not willing to waste one more moment, Jace strode back to the garage. The quicker he got the hell out of here, the better.

Rounding the barn, he rolled up the garage door. He returned his shotgun to its rack near the garage door. He'd like to take it with him, under the circumstances. But he didn't need to risk breaking Wyoming gun laws by having a loaded gun in the truck. Just in case he was pulled over.

Of course, that might be the least of his troubles.

He climbed into his pickup. He didn't glance in the backseat or check the rearview mirror, but he knew she was there. He could smell the light scent of her, some kind of floral shampoo mixed with the metallic tang of fear. "Hold on, this is likely to be a bumpy ride."

UNDERSTATEMENT of the year.

Shanna clung to the floor of the truck, her stomach growing queasier by the moment as the truck bucked and bumped. It was a good thing she hadn't had much for breakfast, because she wouldn't have been able to keep it anyway.

"Here we go."

One big jolt and the truck rolled on comparatively smooth pavement.

Thank God.

"You can sit up now, if you want."

She forced her cramped muscles to unfold. Sliding onto the seat, she looked at the rancher's face in the rearview mirror.

He looked average enough. Shaggy brown hair poked out from under a dark brown cowboy hat. His tanned, thin face sported a day's growth of beard and a healthy number of laugh lines. But his eyes looked wary. As if he didn't quite trust her.

She could hardly blame him. She leaned back and rested her aching neck against the seat. "Thanks. You didn't have to help me."

His eyes flicked up to the rearview mirror. "What's your name?"

Shanna hesitated. She'd been so relieved to escape Barstow and the sheriff, she hadn't given much thought to jumping into a truck with a man she didn't know. But although she really couldn't read what he might be thinking in the mirror's reflection, she didn't feel afraid. Not really.

Maybe at this point she was past fear. "My name is Shanna Clarke."

"Listen, Shanna. I don't know what you're tied up with here, but I suggest you start telling the truth and I suggest you do it now."

So much for her short-lived relief. "I told you the truth."

"People don't try to kill other people for no reason."

"I didn't say he had no reason. I just don't know what his reason is."

He blew out a heavy breath, as if she wasn't telling him what he wanted to hear. As if she was stonewalling on purpose. "I want to help you, Shanna. But you're stretching my patience here."

She didn't know what to say. "I'm telling the truth. I swear."

"The sheriff mentioned that you fired some shots, too."

"Me?" She jolted forward. Pain shot down her neck and gripped her shoulders.

"He said you and your boyfriend had a little argument. That boyfriend wouldn't happen to be Anthony Barstow, would it?"

"No. I don't have a boyfriend. Mr. Barstow is my boss. That's all. I didn't try to shoot anyone. I didn't even fire my gun. Not at deer, not at anything. Not the whole time."

He angled his head to the side, the wide brim of his cowboy hat hiding his face.

She didn't need to see his eyes to feel the skepticism radiate from him in waves. "I know this sounds outrageous. I can't wrap my mind around it myself. But when Mr. Barstow invited me on this trip, I was sure it meant I was getting a promotion. And it wasn't just me. My friend Linda was sure, too. And then this morning, Mr. Barstow started shooting at me."

"And what did you do that made him change from wanting to promote you to wanting to kill you?"

"Nothing! I don't know what changed! I don't know why he's doing this!" She knew she sounded shrill, hysterical, but she couldn't stop. She couldn't calm herself. She couldn't breathe. "You've got to believe me. I don't know why any of this is happening. I'm an accountant. People don't try to shoot accountants."

"Not without reason."

Despair filled her throat, hot and thick, choking her. Why wouldn't he listen? She knew what she was saying didn't make a lot of sense, but she was telling the truth. Why couldn't he see that?

She gripped the seat in front of her, steadying herself. He had listened to her pleas in the garage. She'd seen it in his face. The softening around his jaw. The sympathy in his eyes. And he hadn't told the sheriff where to find her. There had to be something to that, something she could use to reach him now. "You didn't turn me in to Sheriff Gable. You smuggled me out of your ranch. Why?"

He didn't answer.

"You must have believed me." She searched the side of his face she could see under his hat brim, desperate to find that softness, that sympathy, that understanding she'd seen in his expression before.

There was no hint of it.

"Don't you believe me?"

"You haven't given me reason."

She looked away from him and stared through the backseat window at layers of rock and arrowlike spires of lodgepole pine stretching to the horizon and stabbing the sky. Tears fogged her vision, turning the scene into a mosaic of green, gray and blue. She didn't know what more she could say, what more she could do. "Haven't you been listening at all? I don't know why all this is happening. I don't have any reason to give you."

The truck's tires hummed on the two-lane highway. She pressed her fingers to her eyes, wiping away tears. Just this morning she'd been looking forward to the promotion she'd thought was imminent and the raise in pay that would go with it. As she'd ridden her mare through the high mountain valleys, she'd daydreamed of buying a little house with a backyard for Emily. A dream she hadn't dared contemplate since Kurt had left and she'd moved to Wyoming. Maybe they would even have space for a garden. Fresh tomatoes in the summer. Emily loved tomatoes.

Now all those dreams were over. Dead. And she didn't have a clue what would come next.

She looked at the side of the rancher's face, all hard planes and rough stubble. "Where are you taking me?"

"To Copperville."

"Copperville?" She'd only lived in Wyoming a year, but

she knew of the town. It was small, named for an old copper mine long since closed down, and on the other side of Bonner Pass. "Why Copperville?"

"It's across the county line. Different jurisdiction. You can talk to the sheriff there. Let him sort this mess out."

The law. Apprehension fluttered in her stomach. She swallowed hard. The sheriff in another county should be trustworthy, shouldn't he? Of course, until today, she'd believed all law officers were trustworthy.

She shook her head. Maybe she should have known better. After all she'd been through with Kurt, it was shocking she could still believe anyone was who they seemed to be. Not a mistake she was likely to make again. Not after this.

"You have a problem with going to Copperville?"

"No. No problem. Copperville's fine." Since he had offered to take her to Copperville, he must believe a little of her story. At least enough to think she would want help from the law. She was grateful for that.

Unless he'd made the offer merely to test her.

"When you talk to the sheriff in Copperville, keep my name out of it."

His name? "I don't know your name."

His cowboy hat bobbed in a nod. "Let's keep it that way."

She leaned against the back of the seat and strapped on the safety belt. It was all going to be all right. He'd bring her to someone who could help. She might not have the job or the raise or the house, but she was going to make it home in one piece to hug her little girl.

"Oh, hell." The rancher pounded a hand on the steering wheel. "No good deed goes unpunished, does it now?"

She sat up and craned her sore neck, trying to see out the

dusty windshield to the road ahead. Lights flashed red and blue over a rise in the road. "What is it?"

The rancher hit the brakes and swerved to the narrow shoulder. "Roadblock. Seems the sheriff has called in the *real* deputies."

# *Chapter Three*

"We have to turn around. Quick. Go back in the other direction."

Jace clutched the steering wheel until his knuckles ached and met Shanna Clarke's eyes in the rearview mirror. "You really think the sheriff decided to block the highway in only one direction?" Sheriff Gable might be crooked, but that didn't mean he was stupid.

"There has to be another route. A mountain road we can take to get around the deputies. Something."

"Nope. This is a pretty remote area. Nothing but a couple of private ranches and Bonner Pass National Forest." The reason he'd bought land here. Few people to bother him. And everyone was equal under nature's laws.

She pressed back against the seat, snuggling low as if willing herself to disappear. "They're going to find me, aren't they? I'm not going to make it to the county line." Her face glowed white against her bright orange hat. She pressed her lips together so hard they matched the bloodless pale of her cheeks.

He had to look away. This morning all he'd had to worry about was the swelling in his gelding's fetlock and how many steers he could afford to buy come spring. He'd actually believed he could start over, forget the job, forget the law, forget the rich bastards who could buy their way out of any crime. That after seven years, he was a rancher, nothing more. That the slate had finally been wiped clean.

Now he knew all that was nothing but a damn dream.

"How much do you figure Barstow is worth?"

She raised her eyes to meet his. Her eyebrows dipped. A crease dug into her forehead. "What do you mean?"

"How much money does he make in a year? How much does he have in stock options? How much in property? What is he worth?"

"Why are you asking?" Her eyes widened. Her body tensed. She looked like a pronghorn antelope ready to bolt.

"I'm not going to sell you to him, if that's what you're worried about." He waited for some of her tension to ebb.

She showed no sign.

Jace tried to give her a reassuring smile. Maybe he'd grilled her a little hard, trying to get her to abandon her story. But he hadn't had much of a choice. He needed to know she was telling the truth. If he was going to break the law to help her, he had to know he was on the side of right. "How much did he pull in last year? You're an accountant, you say. You should be able to at least give me an educated guess."

"He's worth a lot."

He'd bet. He'd bet it was more than enough to buy off a local sheriff. Probably a judge and a D.A., as well. Even if the bastard succeeded in murdering Shanna Clarke, for whatever the hell reason, he wouldn't serve a day behind bars. He wouldn't even be charged. "What does he have? Twenty mil in stock options? More?"

"I'm not allowed to release numbers."

He almost laughed. Even with the boss trying to kill her, she felt obligated to keep the company's—and her boss's—

secrets. A good, conscientious employee. "You might want to rethink your loyalties. I doubt you still have a job with Talbot. Once your boss starts shooting, you can pretty much kiss any job security goodbye."

She closed her eyes. The stoic slant of her mouth collapsed and her lips began to tremble.

Oh, hell. Sometimes he was too much of a smart-ass for decent people to be around. Another reason he preferred to be alone. Even after all these years, his bitterness was as sharp as a damned knife.

The least he could do was direct that blade in the direction of someone who deserved it. And it was looking more and more like that someone wasn't Shanna Clarke. "I'll get you to Copperville."

She raised wide eyes to meet his. "How?"

"Roads aren't the only way to get around."

"On foot? That's thirty miles."

"Not through Bonner Pass, it's not."

She tilted her head to look out the window at the mountains rising to the east. She looked awed. Maybe frightened was more like it. As if her momma warned her about a wilderness full of big bad wolves and lions, tigers and bears.

Oh, my.

Or maybe she was just picturing them having to bushwhack their way through trees and thick sage with a machete. Or climbing sheer pinnacles of rock with fingers and toes. "There's a trail that skirts around the peaks and crosses over near Bonner Canyon."

"How long will it take?"

"From here? Not long. Maybe a day and a half." His hired hand could take care of his stock for that long. Hell, old Ben probably wouldn't even realize Jace was gone.

"A day and a half of hiking without water?"

"I keep a canteen in the back of the truck in case I break down."

"Food?"

He reached into the glove compartment and pulled out two Snickers bars.

She gave him a skeptical look.

"What do you want? A five-star hotel to stay in? The whole damn sheriff's department is looking for you. You want me to drive down the hill and turn you in, or are you willing to rough it for a few hours to find a sheriff who might be more interested in enforcing the law than lining his pockets?" He paused a beat to let the reality of her situation sink in. "Unless there's something you're not telling…"

She gave her head a tiny shake and raised her chin. "Okay. We walk."

"Good."

He scanned the ridge. On either side of the road, rock and rough scrub fell away to a slope of lodgepole pine and sub-alpine fir. Carefully, he turned the truck on the highway and headed back in the other direction.

"Where are we going?"

"I need to stash my truck. I know a place close to the trail."

"Thanks. For your help. And for believing me. I really do appreciate it."

He could hear the tremble in her voice. Shanna Clarke was scared. Of Barstow. Of Sheriff Gable. Of the wilderness. Probably even of him. And if he was any judge of character, he'd say she was also innocent, which meant it was Barstow who was lying. Barstow who was paying off the sheriff. Barstow who thought he was above the law.

Jace suppressed a chuckle. If Darla knew what he was doing, she would say he was crazy. Maybe she'd be right.

Maybe he was completely out of his mind. But at least he was doing something. And it felt good.

It felt like this time, justice might just have a prayer of coming out on top.

SHANNA KEPT HER EYES focused on the road ahead. The screaming panic that had reverberated through every cell in her body since that first crack of gunfire had finally quieted, at least enough so she could focus on the new mantra she drummed through her mind.

The rancher was going to get her help. It would all be okay.

She had to hold on to that thought. She had to believe it. He seemed like a good enough guy, if a bit gruff and cynical. He seemed as if he knew what he was doing. After all she'd been through, trusting anyone to be what they seemed felt like a risky move.

Too bad she had so few alternatives.

He pulled the truck onto a long gravel road leading to a steel garage. Truck hulls, piles of old tires and rusted-out cars cluttered every square inch. A tall, chain-link fence surrounded the whole mess, a faded sign proclaiming the place Walker's Salvage.

Judging from the look of the place, there wasn't a lot to be salvaged.

She glanced at the rancher out of the corner of her eye. "You're leaving your truck at a junkyard?"

He gave a curt nod, his profile as hard and rugged as the mountain ridges outside the truck's window. "I know the guy who owns it. We can meet up with the Bonner Canyon trail up near that ridge." He pointed to the eyesore's stunning backdrop of gray rock and evergreen.

She brought her attention back to the much less stunning

mess on the other side of chain-link. "It looks closed. It looks deserted."

"Good for us. With the place closed, no one would know when I left it. And no one will spot you."

"How do we get in?"

He stopped the pickup in front of the fence and threw it into Park. Twisting in his seat, he looked at her full on. "I said I know the guy." She waited for him to turn back around, but he didn't. He just watched her as if sizing her up.

A warm tremor jittered through her. Something in between attraction and fear, neither due to his physical appearance. Not that he was bad-looking—if she'd met him under different circumstances, she probably would have found him hot. But there was something about him much more powerful than the lines of a handsome face. Something hard and focused in the way he was looking at her. Something that made her suspect he had his own plan, and she was only a small part.

She shifted in her seat. She knew she should say something, not just sit and stare. But for the life of her, she couldn't think of a single word.

"When we reach Copperville, you can't tell the sheriff about any of this. Not about me helping you. Not about leaving the truck at this junkyard. None of it."

She knew she should just nod, but she couldn't manage to bite back the question. "Why not?"

"Because helping someone evade the law is a crime, and I don't want that crime traced back to me." He leaned toward her, drilling into her with dark eyes. "I'm sticking my neck out for you, Shanna. You have no idea how far. I don't want it coming back to burn me."

She nodded. Tension compounded the throb in her neck. She knew he was taking a risk. And she appreciated it. But as much as she wanted to believe he was doing it out of the goodness of his heart, she was more sure than ever he wasn't. He had his own reasons for getting involved. And judging from his earlier questions, those reasons seemed to have something to do with Mr. Barstow's money. "I don't have any access to Talbot money."

He studied her under his hat brim. His lips stretched into a grin. "I get it. That's why you think I'm helping you. To get a hold of those millions your boss has squirreled away."

"Isn't it?"

"No."

"Then why?"

"You really want to know?"

Did she? "Yes."

He raised a hand and tilted his hat back on his head. "I'm sick of people like your boss doing anything they damn well please and getting away with it. I'm sick of justice only holding sway over the guy who can't afford to write a big enough check."

"That's it? Idealism?"

"I don't seem like an idealist to you?"

"Frankly, no." He seemed harder than that. Darker. A cynic.

"Then just chalk it up to revenge. If I can prove Anthony Barstow tried to kill you, I can make him pay."

Shanna frowned. That didn't feel right, either, at least not entirely. The rancher had given no sign of knowing Mr. Barstow any better than anyone in the state knew Mr. Barstow. Whatever he felt about her boss, it couldn't be personal. And yet, the focus and determination she saw in the line of his jaw and the piercing quality of his eyes had *personal* written all over it.

A dark brow crooked over those piercing eyes. "Is that all, or is there more you want to ask?"

There was a lot more she wanted to ask, but she had the feeling the answers weren't the kind of thing he would willingly give up. And in light of her situation, risking his willingness to help wouldn't be smart. "That's all."

"Good. We're burning daylight. We need to be on our way." He turned back around, swung out of the truck and strode to the gate. In short order he opened the padlock, unlatched the gate and pulled it wide. He climbed back into the truck and drove it inside. Then he closed the gate behind them, not bothering to lock it.

He climbed back in the truck and shifted into gear. The truck dipped and bucked over the rough yard. He drove around to the back of the two-bay steel building and fitted the truck between another pickup and a compact car that's engine had probably given out trying to make it through the mountains.

"This will do." He got out. Reaching across the seat, he grabbed the Snickers bars and stuffed them into his coat pocket. He slammed the door and circled to the back of the truck.

Shanna climbed out of the backseat and followed, catching up in time to see him secure a canteen to his belt and stuff a map and compass in his pocket alongside the candy bars. He turned away from the truck and started back in the direction of the gate.

The junkyard was even more of a mess close-up. The thick and heavy odor of oil seemed to choke oxygen from the air. Quite a feat under the wide-open sky of Wyoming. A bad feeling slid over Shanna. A tingle at her nape, as if they were being watched by malevolent eyes. She shivered and pulled her coat tighter around her neck. The faster they got out of this place, the better.

"You ready?"

She had just opened her mouth to answer when she heard a low growl. She turned slowly and stared into a Doberman pinscher's black eyes.

## Chapter Four

The Doberman's lips curled back from sharp, white teeth. Jace turned slowly, careful not to look into the animal's eyes. When the hell did Walker get a dog?

Jace eyed Shanna. He could feel her tension, sense her desire to bolt. The worst mistake she could make. "Don't move. Don't look him in the eye. And don't let him know you're afraid." Easier said than done.

"What *do* we do?"

What he wouldn't give for his shotgun. It wouldn't be easy, pulling the trigger on a dog, but when it was a choice between that and being mauled... Too bad he didn't have that choice to make. "Back away. Slowly."

They took a step backward together. Then another. "Take it easy, pooch," he said, trying to keep his voice confident and relaxed. "We're not here to steal any of your valuable treasures."

A choked laugh bubbled from Shanna's throat.

Probably hysteria, but what the hell. "Better to laugh than cry."

"I guess."

"Keep backing away. Slow and easy." Jace crooned to the

dog as they took step after step, drawing ever closer to the gate.

"Is he going to attack when we try to leave?"

"As long as we don't turn our backs or make any sudden moves, we should be okay."

He felt her glance, as if she knew he was talking off the top of his head but didn't want to call him on it. She probably wanted to believe he knew what he was talking about. God knew *he* wanted to believe it.

He groped behind his back. His fingers touched wire. A step to the side and he found the latch. "I'll swing it open. You slip through."

"Okay."

"You need to move quickly. Once you move, he might attack."

"What about you?"

"I'll try to block him with the gate." And pray the snarling beast was more eager to chase them out of his yard than really sink his teeth. "Ready?"

"Yes. Ready."

He grasped the cold steel and flipped it up.

The growling crescendoed, but the animal stood his ground.

So far, so good. "Okay. Out the gate. On three."

She took a deep breath, like a swimmer about to dive.

"One…two…" Jace planted his feet and turned to the side.

The dog lunged before he hit three.

Shanna moved with the dog, not back and out the fence as he'd ordered, but toward the animal. Her leg flashed out. Her foot connected with the beast's shoulder.

The dog stumbled back, knocked off balance. Kicking up dust, he scrambled back onto his feet.

Jace grasped Shanna's arm. She was in front of him now,

between him and the dog. Using all his strength, he whirled her around and shoved her toward the open gate.

Jace felt the force of the dog plow into them. He heard Shanna's grunt of pain, heard fabric tear.

He pushed her through and grabbed the gate. Bolting through himself, he closed it just as teeth clanged against chain-link.

He slid the latch into place and spun to Shanna.

She lay half-sprawled in the gravel. A tear ran from her knee to the bottom of her canvas hunting pants.

"Damn, damn, damn." He fell to his knees beside her. His fingers shook. He gripped the sides of tattered fabric and spread them apart.

Her leg jolted, nearly ripping the canvas from his hands.

"Hold still." He tried to be more gentle, to will his hands steady. He pulled the fabric back, exposing her skin.

Skin colored with purple and red blotches in the pattern of dog's teeth.

He suppressed a groan and studied her calf muscle more closely. Bruising. But no punctures. Not that he could see. Her tough, insulated hunting pants saved her that.

Too bad they couldn't have saved her the pain he was sure went with that nasty bruise. Too bad *he* couldn't have saved her that. "I didn't know Walker had a dog."

She nodded her understanding. Eyes and lips pinched with pain, she looked down at her leg. "He didn't break the skin, did he?"

"No. Just a bruise."

She moved into a sitting position and leaned forward, examining the wound herself. "It feels like he ripped the bottom of my leg off."

He frowned, another wave of guilt lapping at his conscience. "Why did you do that? I told you to get out the damn gate."

"He was going to bite you."

"So he bit you instead. And he almost got me, too."

She shook her head. "I don't know. I didn't think. I just saw him jump and…"

Sacrificed herself.

He looked away from her, staring out at the mountains. Not many people would do what she did, move toward trouble in order to save someone they'd just met. Maybe he'd underestimated her. He had to admit, even before her stunt at the gate, the way she'd kept her cool in front of the snarling dog had impressed him. Maybe there was more to what he was doing here than revenge.

Maybe this woman was worth helping all on her own.

A small cloud of dust floated up from the dry grass and scrub near the highway. The kind of dust kicked up by a moving vehicle.

Jace's gut tightened. He looked down at Shanna. "Can you walk?"

"I don't know. Maybe."

"You're going to have to."

She stiffened. "Someone's here?"

He squinted at the source of the dust. The vehicle looked like a light-colored SUV, and despite the distance, he could swear something was written on the side. "Sheriff."

A gasp broke from Shanna's lips. She struggled to push herself up from the dirt and gravel.

He scooped his hands under each arm and lifted her to her feet.

She tested the leg, grimacing.

He slipped an arm around her, supporting her weight. "Run."

He led her back, circling the fence, using the chain-link as a screen between them and the SUV. The dog followed, snarling and growling. So much for hiding. Whoever was in that sheriff's vehicle—deputy or sheriff himself—he'd likely check out what was giving the dog such a fit. They had to get out of here. Across the field and away before the vehicle reached the junkyard.

He grabbed a glance behind.

The SUV was closing fast.

There was no way they'd make it. Not unless they moved more quickly than this.

Jace slipped his arms free. "Get on my back." He leaned down in front of her as if offering a kid a horsey-back ride.

She gripped his shoulders. With a little grunt, she jumped up and clung to his back.

He gripped a leg in each arm and ran. He raced across the open field, heading for a stand of cottonwood, orange and gold blazing against the dark spires of pine.

Shanna's weight bounced at first. She gripped tighter, pulling herself closer, pressing her soft, warm body into his back.

He plunged into the trees, not slowing his stride. He ran, picking his way over felled trees and around clumps of brush until he reached the barren understory of young lodgepole pine. Panting, he stopped and lowered Shanna to the ground. He searched her face, wanting to make sure she was okay.

Her skin was pale. It glowed in the shadow of the forest, as bright as the orange beacon of her hat and coat.

Damn. He hadn't thought about the hat and coat. He swiped the hat off her head. "Coat."

She shrugged out of her coat.

Jace didn't have to look hard to see she was trembling, even though her skin glistened with the slight sheen of sweat. He reached a hand into each sleeve, pulled them inside out and handed the coat back.

She pulled it back on, the deep green lining now facing outward. "Do you think they spotted us? My coat?"

"We'll know soon enough. We'd better put some distance behind us. At least that way, they probably won't be able to follow our trail without dogs."

She shuddered at the mention of man's best friend. "Let's go, then. I think I can walk for a bit, let you rest your back."

"You're a tough one, aren't you?" He pulled off his glove and raised a hand, wiping a thick strand of hair back from her cheek. His fingertips vibrated with the softness of her skin and hair. He knelt down to take a look at her leg.

Her calf looked like hell, mottled red and blue. "Are you sure you can put weight on it?"

She did, unsuccessfully stifling a hiss that escaped through her teeth. "I can walk. At least for a while."

"You don't weigh much. I can carry you."

"Up the mountain?" She shook her head. "Maybe in a while. Right now it's stiffening up. If I don't do some walking, you're going to have to carry me all the way."

He rose to his feet. "Fair enough."

They set out through the easier going of the pine forest. Shanna kept up, staying right beside him despite the fact that her leg had to be throbbing like hell. She was tough, far tougher than she looked. And from what he could see, she was worth a thousand guys like Anthony Barstow. And the law officers they bought.

Wordlessly, they kept moving. The pitch grew steeper. The forest grew sparse. Scrub brush and rock filled in where trees left off. Dense and hard to negotiate. Sweat trickled between Jace's shoulder blades.

An hour passed in near silence, nothing but the sound of

labored breathing in the cool air. Then two hours. The sun moved across the broad sky.

They picked their way upward, winding through gray boulders as big as trailer homes. Even though the fall brilliance of aspen had begun to wane, their yellow leaves still throbbed bright against the dark, straight spires of lodgepole pine. Sharp peaks of gray rock rose far above them, jutting into the sky.

Finally they reached a clear spot. Down a slope, skirting along the crest of a ridge, a dirt path wound over rock and threaded through scrub. "The trail."

"Where?"

Jace let out a heavy breath and came to a halt. He pointed out the trail below. "The worst going's behind us. Most of it's downhill from here. Rest?"

Shanna nodded and collapsed onto a step of lichen-covered rock.

For a while, both just focused on catching their breaths. Shanna was the first to speak. "How did they know where we are?"

"We don't know that they do." Throughout their hike, he'd been keeping his ears open for the sounds of pursuit, the baying of bloodhounds, any sign that they'd been spotted. He hadn't noticed anything. "That deputy could have just been checking out the area. There isn't much between my place and the roadblock. They might have been searching every place you could have gone."

"I hope so." She rubbed the side of her neck, flinching from her own touch as if her leg wasn't the only injury she'd sustained.

"You okay?"

"I will be."

He hadn't been kidding earlier, when he'd said she was

tough. He got the feeling that even if she wasn't okay, she'd will it to be so.

He lowered himself to the rock next to her and squinted out at the afternoon sun. "Jace."

"Excuse me?"

He turned to look at her. "My name, Jace Lantry." He held out a hand.

She took his offered hand, giving a firm shake. "Nice to meet you, Jace."

Yeah, nice. "I only wish it could have been under better circumstances."

Somewhere behind them, a branch snapped.

Jace bolted to his feet. Adrenaline buzzed along his nerves, making everything seem sharp. The distant call of magpie. The whistle of wind around rock. The faraway shush of a waterfall. No hum of voices. No hint of dogs.

He couldn't have failed to notice someone pursuing him. Could he?

Another twig cracked, followed by the shuffle of stone.

The sound wasn't from behind. It was in front. He squinted down the slope toward the trail, staring past rock and into shadow. Trying to see what had made the noise…what he had missed.

## Chapter Five

"What is it?" Shanna whispered, barely able to hear her words over the pounding of her heart.

Jace held up a hand, signaling quiet. He turned around, once again peering under his hat brim in the direction of the sun. The corner of his mouth quirked into a dry smile. "Looks like we're going to have to take the long way."

Not following, she shot him a questioning frown.

He nodded down the slope.

She followed the gesture with her gaze. All she could see was the path he'd pointed out winding along the rock-strewn ridge. "The trail?"

"Not that. Closer."

She raised her hand, shielding her eyes from the sun. Something moved in the shadow of a large rock. It stopped… and looked at them.

A trill of fear ran through her. A bear. And judging from the size and bushy, blond-tipped coat, it was a grizzly.

She'd heard stories about grizzlies. Horror stories of attacks. Amusing stories of bear antics. Awe-inspiring stories about up-close sightings. They all spun together in her mind until she wasn't sure what to think. And she sure didn't know what to do. "Jace?"

"She's seen us, so for the time being, we just sit still."

"What if she comes closer?"

"Then we sit even more still."

That didn't sound like much fun. At this point, she didn't even know if she could force herself to remain in one place if the bear approached. Her body might just take off running without any input from her. "Is it true, about grizzlies? Do they charge?"

"Not usually."

"But sometimes?"

"I've never been close enough to one to find out."

"That wasn't what I was hoping to hear."

He chuckled, but even though he might be acting cool, he sounded less than relaxed. "If she charges, there's a chance it's just a bluff."

"So we call her bluff? I don't like that picture. What if it's not a bluff?"

"Drop to the ground and roll up in a ball."

She pulled her gaze from the bear and focused on Jace. "You're kidding, right?"

"Not even a little."

She swallowed, her throat tight, and turned back to the grizzly. The animal was still cloaked in shadow, but she seemed closer, as if she were ambling this way. "Is it my imagination, or is she coming up the slope?"

"It's not your imagination."

The bear broke in to the waning sunlight. She was larger than Shanna had originally thought, her head bigger than most horses' she'd seen. Her shaggy coat rolled as she walked. Her belly hung low with fat stored up for winter.

"I don't want to wait to see her at close range."

She could hear Jace's coat shuffle. "Maybe we don't have to."

She turned her head.

He held the two Snickers bars aloft. "This is probably what she smells. Why she's coming up here."

Looking at the bars, Shanna's mouth had the audacity to water. Before they'd left the truck, she'd thought candy bars to be barely sufficient, as far as food was concerned. Now that she hadn't eaten since daybreak and had been running nearly all day, they seemed precious. Life-sustaining. A delicacy her body craved.

Apparently the bear craved them, too.

And Shanna wasn't about to fight for them. "Give them to her."

"Exactly what I had in mind." He slowly raised a hand to point to one side of where the bear approached. "When I toss these, I want you to walk slowly in that direction. We'll circle around to the trail from below."

She could see what he meant by taking the long way. "On three?"

"On three. Slowly, remember? We don't want her to think we're prey trying to escape."

Wasn't that exactly what she was? If not to the bear, to Mr. Barstow and the county sheriff's department.

"Ready?"

"Ready."

"One…two…three." He tossed the chocolate toward the bear and to the opposite side of their escape route. And grasping Shanna's hand, the two of them started their slow-motion retreat.

Shanna's side ached. Her legs wobbled. Her breath rasped in her ears, yet as hard and fast as she panted, she couldn't seem to get enough air.

The detour around the grizzly had amounted to two extra

hours of cutting through thick brush and climbing a slope of ankle-twisting talus. She could no longer differentiate the pain in her calf from the ache of exhausted muscles. She no longer thought about her neck at all.

She wanted to stop. To sit. To rest. But thoughts of the grizzly and the sheriff's trolling SUV kept her moving her feet forward. Copperville had to be close. It had to be. She didn't know how much more of this she could take.

By the time they'd gotten back to the trail, the sun had already dipped low in the sky. As they hiked along the ridge, she kept her eyes focused on the trail in front of her, on Jace's boots, on nothing. The mountainside that had once awed her with its beauty felt cold and hard and unforgiving. The sky that had seemed so wide and majestic had darkened to gray as twilight closed in.

The bugling of bull elk rang off rocks, echoing from valleys below. A cross between a melodic whistle and a guttural bellow, the sound felt melancholy to Shanna. Lonely. A plaintive mating cry.

"Would you look at that." Jace stopped in front of her.

She almost ran in to him. She lifted her gaze from the trail and focused on his face. It took her a second to process the unfamiliar expression, the strange light in his eyes. "What is it?"

He pointed to the horizon.

She followed the gesture, over layers of rough terrain, to the brilliance of the sky.

Shanna almost forgot to breathe. A moment ago the vista had felt harsh and imposing. Now it was lit with the fire of angels. She sucked in a long breath.

"It's something, isn't it?" The glow she'd seen in his eyes radiated from his voice. "That's one reason I moved here. These sunsets can sustain a man."

She couldn't disagree. She might not have moved to Wyoming for any reason so poetic, but that didn't mean she couldn't appreciate the state's beauty. Even if a moment ago, she'd been beat down by its brutality. "It's gorgeous."

He looked away from the sunset and focused on her. For a moment he didn't say anything, he just watched her. Then he nodded abruptly as if breaking away from a spell. "We need to find a place to hunker down for the night."

A jitter she didn't think she still had the energy to feel centered in her chest. As if in looking out over the expansive sunset together, she had shared something intimate with this man she barely knew. A man who was now looking for a place to spend the night.

Her exhaustion must be warping her brain. "How close are we to Copperville?"

"Close."

"Then can't we keep moving?" She knew the jitter she felt was ridiculous. But that wasn't her only concern. The sooner she could reach safety, the better. Even if she had to walk all night.

He shook his head. "We need to make it down the ridge to Bonner Canyon. We're not likely to do that in the dark."

"But staying here can't be all that safe. What about… animals?"

As if on cue, a coyote howled, the sound's source uncomfortably close.

He nodded in its direction. "Coyotes are noisy, but they aren't going to mess with us."

"I was thinking of bears."

"They won't find us very interesting anymore. We're no longer carrying any of that five-star cuisine." He gave her a teasing grin.

Shanna found herself smiling back. She touched a hand to

her stomach. "Thanks for reminding me." She looked back to the vanishing sun.

She couldn't figure out Jace Lantry. How could he be so cynical and brusque one moment and yet wax poetic about the sky and warmly tease her the next?

Not that she'd ever been good at figuring out men. Nor was she interested in figuring out this one. He was helping her, and for that, she was grateful. Her jitters were likely just fatigue… and hunger.

Jace strode away, leaving her gaping at the sunset like a tourist. She scrambled to catch up.

He walked to a rock face that angled outward at the top, forming a shallow shelf. Bending down, he pulled brush away from the rock's base. "Here. It might not be one of those cushy hotel beds, but this will do."

Shanna looked at the tiny space. "It's kind of small."

He shot her a dry look, as if he thought she was kidding. "You'll like the close quarters when the temperature drops."

The temperature was already dropping. She could see her breath cloud in the air when the angle of the setting sun was right.

Maybe he had a point.

He grunted and crouched down slowly, the first sign he'd shown that he might be as stiff and tired as she was. He fitted his back against the wall of rock and gestured to the spot next to him.

She hesitated.

"I don't bite. I know it might not have seemed that way back in the truck. But in my defense, we didn't meet under the best of circumstances."

Shanna let out a breath she hadn't known she was holding. She forced herself to crouch down and fit her body into the tiny space next to him. Her side touched his from shoulder to hip. "There."

He watched her, his face close enough for her to see the few silver hairs glinting among the rough stubble on his chin and cheeks. Light lines fanned out from the corners of his eyes. He was probably older than she'd previously thought.

"How long have you been a rancher?"

"I bought my place a few years ago."

"How many?" As well as he seemed to know the land, she'd assumed he'd lived here all his life.

"About five."

"What did you do before that?"

"It's not important."

"It's important to me."

"Why?"

"I don't know. After all you've done to help me, I guess I just feel I should know something about you."

"You know I'm not going to hurt you. You know I'm at least trustworthy enough to get you to Copperville. That's all you need to know."

He was probably right. Then why did she still feel the need to know more? Unless she just wanted to avoid the silence between them, a silence that seemed more intimate than words.

"The person you need to focus on is yourself," he said.

"Me?"

"How are you a threat to Anthony Barstow?"

"A threat? I'm not a threat."

"Then why does your boss want to kill you? Why is the sheriff's department after you?"

A threat. She hadn't thought about it that way. She still couldn't wrap her mind around the whole idea. How could Mr.

Barstow want to kill her? How could someone like her be a threat to him? "It doesn't make sense."

"It must make sense to him. Think, Shanna. There has to be a reason. People don't just pick up rifles and start shooting."

Her head ached. Her leg throbbed. A hitch lodged in her lower rib cage, a pain like a needle piercing her with each breath. "I don't know why Mr. Barstow would shoot at me. I don't know why the sheriff is after me. I just…don't know."

"I think you do."

She stared at him.

"Think."

She searched her memory. She'd never had anything but glowing job evaluations. She'd moved smoothly up the company ladder. She and Linda had both been sure the invitation to the hunting trip would lead directly to an invitation into management. She shook her head.

"Is there something personal between you?"

It took her a second to realize what he was suggesting. "Between me and Mr. Barstow? He's married."

He crooked a brow. "It's been known to happen."

"No. Absolutely not."

"Did he *want* something to happen between you? Did you turn him down?"

Mr. Barstow had always been nice to her, in his brusque way. But she'd never gotten the impression that he'd been interested in anything other than her doing her job. "No. There was nothing like that."

He frowned, as if her answer wasn't good enough, as if he didn't believe her.

"I'm not dating anyone, least of all Mr. Barstow. I mind my own business. I'm a good employee. People don't try to kill people like me. I'm an accountant, for crying out loud."

Frustration and exhaustion washed over her in a wave. Tears stung her sinuses and made her vision blur. It still felt so unreal. How had this happened? How had she gone from mild-mannered accountant to woman on the run? And how could she wake up from this nightmare and return to her quiet life?

"You're an accountant."

"Yes."

"So you deal with the financial end of the company."

"Yes." She could see where he was going. "You think this has to do with money?"

"Does it?"

"I've racked my brain, and I can't figure out how. I haven't worked on anything out of the ordinary. I haven't seen any numbers that were somehow…off."

"Are you sure? If Barstow has been skimming off the top…"

She shook her head. "I'm sure. Mr. Barstow is not embezzling from the company."

Jace gave her a sideways glance. "People can come up with some pretty creative ways to skim. Ways that are tough to detect."

"Don't I know it." She almost laughed. "My ex-husband embezzled from the company where he worked, among other things. I've spent the last two years trying to help the authorities sort out the mess he made."

"Your ex-husband. Might this have something to do with him?"

Shanna shut her eyes against another surge of emotion battering against her frayed nerves. During the long hours of hiking, she'd been raking her memory for some reason Mr. Barstow wanted her dead, picking apart every word he'd ever said to her, analyzing every syllable she'd said back. She hadn't come up with a thing. Now having Jace pelting her with question after question was making her head feel as if it was about to explode. "Barstow never even knew my ex. I took the job at Talbot and moved to Palmer after my divorce."

"Where are you from?"

"St. Louis." She shook her head. She was done answering questions. She didn't want to think about Kurt or St. Louis or her meeting last week with the SEC agent. She'd had enough of Kurt's mess. She didn't want to think about him anymore. Except for Emily, of course, she wanted all traces of her marriage to him to go away.

Too bad she couldn't dismiss Mr. Barstow so easily.

Or Jace. He refused to tell her anything about himself, yet she had the feeling he wouldn't stop until he'd unearthed every humiliation in her past, whether it had to do with the trouble she was in now or not. "I'm tired. I need to sleep. Unless you feel like sharing your life story."

He looked up at the sky, not bothering to answer.

Of course not. Secrecy seemed to be a way of life with men...at least any man she'd tried to trust lately. They all had something to hide. None were what they seemed.

And she couldn't help but wonder who Jace Lantry really was.

She followed Jace's gaze up to the sky. More stars than seemed possible sparkled against the darkness, turning the night into layers of shadow. Shanna pulled in a breath of cold air. The Wyoming sky made her feel small, her problems insignificant. And at least in that, she could grasp a sliver of hope.

She rested her head on the rock wall behind her. The plaintive howl of coyotes echoed off rock and disappeared into the vast sky. The wind picked up, ripping through the ridges and precipices above them, adding its wail to the coyote's.

Shanna shivered. As tired as she was, she doubted she

would sleep. Not with Barstow out there hunting her. Not with the entire sheriff's department assisting him. Not holed up with a man who was little more than a stranger, a man who shifted from kindness to secrecy with the unpredictability of a mountain wind.

THE WIND PICKED UP just before dawn, and with it came an unmistakably sharp scent. Jace tilted his head back. No stars to the west. Not a good sign.

He slipped his arm out from behind Shanna and thrust himself to his feet. He stepped as close to the edge of the ridge as he dared in the dim light and waited for the sun. As pink crested the east horizon, he scanned the area down ridge. Lodgepole pine, Englemann spruce and subalpine fir towered in thick clumps where rock sloped down into the canyon. Downed logs piled beneath them on the slope like a spilled box of toothpicks. Beyond the trees, the water of Bonner Lake reflected tumultuous clouds. They had a good two miles to reach the trail that rimmed Bonner Canyon. Already dark clouds shrouded the peaks to the west, lightning illuminating them in flashes. If they had any hope of making it before the storm hit full force, they'd better get a move on.

"How far do we have left to go?"

He started a little at her voice. He hadn't heard her come up behind him. His powers of observation must be rusty. That, or yesterday's exhaustion was taking its toll. "How far to Copperville? I'd guess about six miles, give or take."

"Oh, thank God."

He knew what she was thinking. Six miles was nothing compared to the distance they'd traveled yesterday. He needed to warn her. "The first four aren't going to be easy."

"None of it's been easy."

"Compared to what's ahead, everything we've done so far was."

The little crease between her eyebrows that he'd noticed the day before dug deep. "You said it was all downhill."

"It is. But the path is tricky." He hated to add to it, but she needed to know what they faced. "And snow is moving in."

She looked up at the sky. "Let's get going, then."

He stole another peek at the rushing clouds, heavy and dark. His thoughts exactly.

Having nothing to eat for breakfast even if they'd wanted it, which he sure as hell did, they set off down the trail. The first snow hit before they'd walked a quarter mile. Flakes whipped past them, big as pebbles. They swirled in the conflicting air currents rushing over the ridge. They settled into crevices, bringing out the texture of rock like powder in a fingerprint.

"It's beautiful," Shanna yelled over the rushing wind. "Like the mountains are dusted with sugar."

He doubted she'd think that for long.

Little by little, sheets of blowing snow blotted out the sun. The vista before them turned shades of gray. Wet rock faces took on the dull gleam of pewter. Wind howled through the ridges and peaks of rock above.

Jace concentrated on the ground beneath his feet. The trail was there one moment, then swept away by waves of white the next. Snow blew off cliffs, spinning and twirling in the air, making him dizzy. He knew this trail, yet didn't know it. He knew where he was, or did he? He knew where he wanted to go, yet didn't at all.

His boots slipped, snow and ice turning the rock as slick as if it were covered in grease. His muscles burned. His lungs screamed for air. He felt like the rock was shifting under him with the wind, the snow.

He gritted his teeth, tightened his grip on Shanna's hand and plunged ahead. It had to be worse for her. He was used to physical work, used to the mountains, used to the harshness that weather could bring. Shanna was an accountant.

But still, she kept up. Gripping his hand. Her footsteps following his.

He squinted into the swirling gray and white. The shadow of rock loomed above. The flat glint of water. The rumble of a waterfall rose over the scream of the wind.

He knew this place. He'd been here before, many times. And if they were this far, that meant they had made it down the ridge. Bonner Canyon opened below.

They plowed forward. Stones rolled under his feet. Behind him, he could hear Shanna scramble to keep her footing. He reached back, grabbing her other arm to keep her from going down. He steered her into the lee of a boulder.

She searched his eyes. Snowflakes clung to her eyelashes and blended with her hair. The frigid wind colored her cheeks a bright pink. Ridiculously, in the middle of a blizzard with their lives balancing as precariously as scree at the bottom of the canyon, all he could think about was how beautiful she looked.

"You're not going to tell me that was the easy part, are you?" she said.

He sucked in a breath of cold through clenched teeth. "No. That was the hard part."

Her chest fell as if she'd been holding her breath for his answer.

"But the next mile or so is no picnic."

"Too bad. I'm starving." She smiled, but the expression looked as forced as her joke.

He smiled back, the least he could do for her effort at

levity. "We need to follow the rim of the canyon. There's a trail, but it's going to be pretty precarious in this snow."

She squinted ahead. "A trail? How are we going to see it? I can barely see your eyes."

Good damn question. Meandering and ill-defined, the path balanced near the canyon's edge at several points. One wrong step or slip on the quickly accumulating snow, and they'd find themselves plunged into the icy lake below. Not exactly a refreshing dip. If the fall didn't kill them, hypothermia surely would. "At least we can be sure no one will be able to follow."

"Because they would have to be crazy."

Exactly. But he thought better than to voice the confirmation. Shanna had been through a lot of challenges in the past twenty-four hours. Her humor seemed to be holding, but their ordeal wasn't over yet.

"Can't we just stay here until this blows over?"

"We could if we want to risk being trapped up here for a while."

"How long?"

"Hard to say. Could be a few hours. Could be until next spring."

Brow furrowed, she squinted out into the gray world. "Then let's go."

He held out his palm. She placed her hand in his. A surge of heat laced his blood and coursed through his body. Heat of desire and awareness and admiration.

Heat he couldn't let himself feel.

He stepped slowly along the snow-obscured path. He'd better keep his eyes open and tread carefully. One bad step and he'd plunge both of them into a world of hurt.

# Chapter Six

By the time Shanna and Jace made it around the canyon and through the narrow pass to the foothills sloping into Copperville, the mountains were covered in a blanket of white. Shanna's muscles were past burning, past exhaustion, past weakness. Pain had taken up permanent perch in her shoulders and neck. Given a hard cot in a dry room, she could sleep for a week.

The land sloping down to Copperville was shockingly different from the mountains they'd just left. Down here, no sign of snow touched the grass. Instead of the crisp snap of winter, rain-dampened sagebrush perfumed the air. Instead of subalpine forest and canyons, oil rigs and quarries dotted the open range.

Talbot invested in energy interests all over the state, but while Shanna was familiar with the numbers associated with several of the companies in the area, she had never actually visited any of them. She was little more than a stranger.

They walked along a dirt road for several miles before reaching the highway leading to Copperville. The town itself was small. Once an abandoned copper mine, it was now experiencing rapid growth. An energy boomtown, like many others in the area, including her current hometown of Palmer.

Jace veered off the street at a small steel building backing up to the wooded banks of a creek. A sign out front proclaimed the place The White Elephant Store, and from the look of it, it sold secondhand furniture and close-out items. No doubt a popular place with oil-field hands and miners that flooded the area looking for items to furnish their temporary living arrangements.

Jace motioned to Shanna to follow him around the corner of the building. He stopped in a protected area facing the creek.

Shanna scanned the blazing cottonwoods and gurgling water. "Why are we stopping here?"

He gestured across the street. A stone building with smoke-clouded windows sat next to a weed-choked lot that likely wouldn't be vacant long. The Hideout Saloon.

"Appropriate name," she joked.

Jace didn't laugh. "And maybe a good place to gather some information. I'm going in to see what I can learn."

"Okay. Let's go."

"Just me." He held out a hand, blocking her path. "You stay put."

She glanced from Jace to the bar and back again. She didn't understand what he was trying to say. They had crossed the county line. Why would she hover behind a furniture store when she needed to be calling the sheriff? "They probably have a phone. I can call for help."

"It's not that simple."

"Why not?"

"A sheriff can't just call out his deputies like some sort of private army. Not even a crook like Benson Gable. They have some reason to look for you."

"What do you mean?"

"You're not just wanted by your boss now, you're wanted by the law."

"The law?" She knew what he was saying made sense—there had been the roadblock. The deputy's car at the junkyard. But she'd been so focused on getting to Copperville and getting help, it took a moment for her to change gears. "I didn't do anything."

"If Barstow and the sheriff say you did, if they can come up with evidence that you did, then until a court says otherwise, you did. Even in this county. That whole thing about innocent until proven guilty doesn't mean you won't be thrown in jail in the meantime."

"What could they possibly say I did?" She voiced the question, but she already had an idea of the answer. "The lover's spat."

"That's the story Gable gave me. You tried to shoot your boyfriend. Attempted murder."

What a laugh. She hadn't been involved with a man since Kurt left. And her jittery attraction to Jace aside, she didn't intend that to change anytime soon. "Doesn't it matter if their story is a lie?"

"Not if it's tight enough. Not if they can show some sort of evidence."

She gnawed on the inside of her lip and tried to remain calm. She was so close to safety. So close to returning to Emily. So close to ending this nightmare.

"Obviously their first choice was for you to die in a hunting accident. When that didn't work, they figured out another way to bring you down. Shot hunting, shot trying to flee the sheriff's department, it all adds up to the same thing."

Maybe she wasn't so close. "The way you're talking, I can't win. Maybe I should turn myself in to the deputies. They'll at least have to arrest me, instead of just shooting me.

Then I can prove I'm innocent of whatever they're saying I did."

He tilted his head, as if that was a possibility to consider. "Why don't we find out what you're up against first?"

"Okay. But I'm going with you."

"You can't do that. For all we know, your picture is all over television."

He'd warned her about what might happen, but he had yet to give her a reason to hide out like some kind of criminal. She hadn't done anything. She'd had enough of acting as though she had. "So what? If I can't make all of it go away, why shouldn't I at least get it over with as soon as I can?"

He pressed his lips into a grim line. "No one knows I'm helping you."

"And you don't want them to." She got that part. Still, the unease she'd felt during their hike through the mountains gnawed at the back of her neck. There was more to Jace's helping her than met the eye. She was sure of it. "What aren't you telling me?"

"It will only take a few minutes to find out what's going on. You can make your decision after we have some facts."

She shook her head. "That's not good enough. If you want me to wait here for you, you're going to have to tell me why."

He pulled his hat from his head and ran a hand through his hair before clapping the hat back on his head. Pushing a resigned breath through tight lips, he met her eyes. "Because I've done some time in jail. And as soon as they find out I helped you escape the sheriff back at my place, they'll put me right back."

Shanna leaned against the building's corrugated steel siding. She didn't know what she'd expected Jace to say, but it wasn't this. Not at all. "Jail? What for?"

"I crossed a man with a lot of money. I paid the price."

Her mind stuttered, still trying to fit the word *jail* into her impression of Jace. "So that's what you have against Mr. Barstow? He reminds you of someone else? Someone responsible for throwing you in jail?"

"Something like that. Now, are you going to stay put while I find out what's going on or not?"

Shanna crossed her arms over her chest. She'd thought Jace was a lot of things…a cowboy, a mountain man, a cynic. There were times on their trek through the mountains that she'd even wanted him to be a hero. But it never occurred to her he was some kind of criminal. Some kind of jailbird. It just proved what Linda said all along. She was too gullible. Too trusting. Men were never what they seemed. At least not what she wanted them to be. It was time she got used to it.

"Shanna?" He was waiting for an answer.

She bobbed her head in a nod. She wouldn't drag him into her mess. Not any deeper than he was already. It was the least she could do after he'd risked his own skin to get her to Copperville.

He touched her arm. "Are you okay?"

She waved off his concern. "I'm fine. Surprised. After all that's happened, I didn't think I could be anymore. I guess I was wrong."

He opened his mouth, as if he wanted to explain, then closed it without uttering a word.

Maybe it was better that way. Maybe the less she knew, the better off she was. "Don't be long."

JACE PUSHED HIS WAY into the Hideout Saloon and bellied up to the bar. The place smelled like the inside of an ashtray and looked as if it had barely survived until closing time the night before. From the vacant look of things, the locals hadn't gotten off work yet, or maybe they were in the same shape as the bar and had opted to lie low tonight. In the tavern's defense, a Dale Watson song drifted from the corner jukebox.

Jace slid off his coat, still wet from the snow, and slipped it over the stool's vinyl back. Settling in, his gaze landed on the tapper. What he wouldn't give for a cold beer, real country music and an afternoon with nothing to worry about. Instead here he was, flirting with landing himself back in jail all to help a woman with pretty green eyes.

He shook his head and tried to banish the image of Shanna's eyes from his mind. The worst thing was the look she'd given him when he told her he'd done time. Disappointment. Disillusion. He still felt the sting. Maybe he shouldn't care, but he did. And that was more worrisome than anything. He'd agreed to help her in the hope he could finally make a rich bastard pay for his sins. But somewhere along the trek through Bonner Pass, things had gotten complicated.

Jace pulled his gaze from the tapper. This might be the perfect place to drown his sorrows, but that wasn't why he was here. He needed to find out what, if anything, the locals knew about what had happened on Gusset Ridge. Or at least, the sheriff's version of what had happened.

He focused on the big man behind the bar. "Hey."

The bartender looked up from the back bar. "Minute." He turned back to the pressing job of wiping sludge-thick dust off a bottle of Drambuie that looked like it hadn't been splashed into a glass in ten years.

So customer service wasn't this guy's priority.

Jace glanced around the bar's dark interior. He pointed to a television suspended high in one corner. "Can I get you to turn that on?"

The bartender nearly growled. Seemingly in slow motion, he lumbered to the end of the bar and flicked a switch on the wall. A sitcom flickered on the screen.

"Can you turn the channel? I was hoping to catch the news."

You'd think he'd asked the guy to spit-shine his shoes. He glared at Jace. "You drinking something? Or you just come in to watch the tube?"

The sour odor of day-old alcohol on the bartender's breath just about knocked Jace over. "I'll have a tap. You serve food?"

"Kitchen's not open."

Jace's stomach pinched. The stapled paper menu stuck between ashtray and salt-and-pepper shakers promised grub from noon until midnight. But since this guy seemed to be the type to carry out a grudge, Jace thought better of pointing that out. Let the guy nurse his hangover while Jace nursed a beer. He'd stop at the corner store and get some food to bring back to Shanna. "Ran into a roadblock on the highway yesterday. Any idea what that was about?"

The bartender plunked a watery-looking beer in front of him and grunted something unintelligible.

"Sheriff's department," Jace prodded. "Looked like something was going on up Gusset's Ridge way."

"Don't know."

Some help this guy was. Just Jace's luck to get a bartender who hated small talk. He glanced up at the tube where an impossibly gorgeous blonde was arguing with an impossibly preppy actor-type wearing scrubs. "They might have some explanation on the news. Mind changing the channel?"

The guy gave him a nod, yet didn't move one muscle toward the television.

Jace glanced at his watch. Two minutes after five. If the sheriff's roadblock made the news, it would likely be a headlining story. He'd better hurry. "You got a remote?"

"Lost it."

Great. Jace pushed away from the bar and strode to the corner. Climbing up on a stool, he manually changed the channel just as the Action News headline flashed on the screen. He turned up the volume. Pity to drown out the music, especially since it seemed to be the only thing this dump had going for it, but he needed to hear.

After stories ranging from an environmental group protesting a uranium mine in the Red Desert Basin to reports of chronic wasting disease in deer, Jace was rethinking the decision. He must have either missed the report, or there wasn't one.

The door swung open and a stream of early evening sunlight poured into the dingy bar, highlighting streaks on the mirror behind the booze bottles. The bartender glanced up. Instead of the growl he'd given Jace, he broke out a wide grin. "Hey, baby. How you doing?"

Jace would recognize that look anywhere. The wide smile. The too-long stare. The feeling that the whole world came alive when that special person entered a room. He'd looked at Darla like that once. Hell, if he hadn't had his head handed to him, he would have looked at her that way for the rest of his life.

A woman who looked more green around the gills than the bartender plopped on the bar stool next to Jace. "I survived. Wasn't sure I was going to make it this morning."

"Hard day?"

He focused on the weather report and sipped his beer in an attempt to give some semblance of privacy.

"Yeah, thanks to you and those shots of tequila."

The bartender pulled a tap and set a glass of a beer in front of her, still smiling. "A little hair of the dog?"

The woman groaned, but took a sip anyway. "Hey, you hear the excitement?"

"My excitement is you coming in here."

She giggled. "No, I mean, the manhunt."

Jace gave up any interest in the weather report. He fought the urge to lean toward the woman in an effort to catch each word.

"Manhunt?" the bartender repeated.

"Yeah, Susan told me about it. I guess some woman shot her boyfriend."

The bartender grunted. "Yeah? Who's the bitch?"

Jace could see the woman shrug in the mirror's dim reflection. "I don't know. But Susan said the sheriff was stopping cars, looking for her."

"Who's the boyfriend?"

"Some rich guy from Palmer. Davis, I think they said."

The name meant nothing to Jace, although Shanna had mentioned another man was on the hunting trip, Talbot's financial officer.

"She killed him dead."

Jace went cold.

"I guess they were hunting. Had a fight. She shot the outfitter, too."

Jace spun to face the woman. Gut tight, he forced the question from his lips. "The outfitter have a name?"

The bartender glared. "What's it to you?"

Jace ignored him, keeping his focus on the woman. "A name. Did they release the outfitter's name?"

The woman pushed bleached hair the texture of cotton candy over one shoulder and smiled as if enjoying the attention and not willing to give it up too quickly. "I'm so bad at names."

Jace gritted his teeth. He didn't have time for this. He needed to know. He wanted to shake her. "Was it Roger Harris? Gusset Ridge Outfitters?"

She screwed up her forehead, then reluctantly nodded. "That sounds right…maybe…"

Jace felt sick. He wasn't close with Roger. Hell, he'd bought the ranch so he wouldn't have to be close with anybody. But he liked Roger. He was a good man. Honest. Kind. Too kind.

He didn't deserve to die.

Jace's ears hummed, anger churning in him like a river over rapids. He threw a few bucks on the bar, slipped off his stool and made for the door. He tried to look as casual as possible, but he could feel the bartender's eyes on him even after the door closed.

And he couldn't help but wonder how long it would take the guy to pick up the phone.

## Chapter Seven

Cigarette smoke wafted toward Shanna, carried on a wave of giggles.

Apparently she and Jace weren't the only ones to discover the great hiding place behind the furniture store. So had what was probably the town's entire preteen girl population—all four of them. The cigarette butts littering the ground should have clued her in.

Shanna lowered herself between a scraggly clump of bushes and the store's steel siding. She didn't know how long Jace had been gone, but it seemed like forever. Even so, her mind was still buzzing with his confession and what it might mean.

She closed her eyes and leaned her head back against the steel. She was such a damn romantic. As starry-eyed as those girls puffing on cigarettes and dreaming of cute boys. Would she ever learn? Men were who they were, not who she wanted them to be. All her romantic ideals—the loving husband, the wise boss, the valiant cowboy—were fantasies.

She needed to start facing reality.

She scraped the hair out of her eyes. She'd give Jace a few more minutes, then she was going to the sheriff and taking her chances. She hadn't done anything wrong. She didn't have anything to fear.

Men's voices rumbled from the street.

Shanna peered around the corner of the building.

A sheriff's vehicle sat in front of the tavern. A man and a woman stood on the sidewalk outside, talking to the deputy. The man gestured dramatically to the tavern with a meaty hand.

Shanna's throat tightened. She tried to make out their words over the throb of her pulse. Something had happened. But what?

One of the men glanced her way.

She ducked back behind the building. Every nerve in her body screamed to run.

The excitement had to be about her. The odds of a sheriff's car stopping outside the very tavern where Jace had gone to gather information were too great for even her to believe it was a coincidence. So what had happened? Where was Jace?

*Had he turned her in? Would he do that?*

She took another peek around the corner, careful to keep at the same level as the bushes to conceal her presence. Still just the man, the deputy and the woman. No Jace.

*So where was he?*

She pushed horrible images from her mind. Jace arrested. Jace dead. She had to concentrate. She had to figure out what to do next.

"Shanna."

She started. Her empty stomach lurched. She squinted into the shadows, searching the thick copse of cottonwood and willow that flanked the creek.

"Shanna. Here."

She followed the sound of his voice to a parking lot nestled behind the convenience store on the other side of the schoolgirls' smoking refuge. The girls looked from the parking lot to her, staring with big, watchful eyes.

At first she just saw the truck, a rusted-out pickup that had seen better decades. Then Jace propped an arm and leaned out the open window. "Hurry."

Shanna shot to her feet. Pushing past the surprised girls, she raced across the parking lot to the truck. She didn't know what was going on, what he'd learned or where the pickup had come from. For all she knew, she was a fool to trust him. But she didn't think so. He'd gotten her this far, hadn't he? Jail or no jail, Jace had to be a better bet than a sheriff she didn't know.

She yanked open the passenger door and jumped inside. "Where did you get this truck?"

"Bought it." Jace jammed the truck into gear. "Get down."

She slid off the seat and onto the floorboards, folding her body so the top of her head was below window level.

Jace hit the gas. The truck's engine vibrated under her and growled loudly enough to rattle her teeth. He took a hard turn and the truck jolted onto the street.

"What's going on?" Shanna asked more forcefully.

"You tell me."

"What?"

"What happened on Gusset Ridge?"

"I told you what happened."

"I want details."

"Details? What do you mean?"

"Did you fire your gun?"

"No."

"Sure about that?"

"Of course I'm sure."

"Where is it?"

"What?"

"Your rifle. I assume you weren't out hunting deer without a rifle."

Her rifle. What had happened to it? For a moment, she couldn't think. She couldn't breathe.

Jace took a hard left, forcing her to hang on to the seat.

"It was in its holster thing. On my saddle."

"And what happened to the horse?"

"I fell off. She was scared. She took off and joined the pack mules."

"So you didn't even touch the rifle? Didn't return fire? Didn't even try to protect yourself?"

"I loaded it. After that the gun wasn't anywhere near me. By the time I realized Mr. Barstow was shooting at me, my horse was long gone."

Jace set his chin. From her angle below the dash, she could see a muscle working in his throat. "Two men were killed on that ridge."

"Two men? Killed?" Somehow she couldn't believe it. Here she'd been shot at, Barstow had tried to kill her, but the idea that someone had actually died yesterday shocked her to the core. "Who?"

"My neighbor, for one."

"The outfitter?"

"Roger Harris. Good man. One of the finest I've met since I moved here."

She remembered him. He was nice. Considerate. He'd helped her saddle her horse that morning. "I'm sorry."

"For what? You said you didn't kill him."

His tone was so sharp, she reeled backward, pressing her back against the door. "I didn't. I'm telling the truth."

He clenched his teeth and took another turn. He pressed his foot to the accelerator. The truck shuddered but responded. The engine roared. The tires whistled over pavement.

Shanna didn't know what to think. She didn't know what to do. Jace's anger, his obvious belief that she'd kept a horrible truth from him, scared her. She could only hope he would tell her all of what he'd learned and give her a chance to explain... and that he'd believe her. "You said two men died. Who was the second?"

"A guy by the name of Davis. Know him?"

Ron Davis? She felt a shock zing through her, then nothing but numbness. "He's Talbot Mining's chief financial officer. He was part of our hunting party."

"How did he end up dead?"

"I—I don't know. Mr. Barstow must have shot him, and your neighbor, too." She gave her head a little shake to clear it. She still couldn't wrap her mind around the image of Mr. Barstow as a killer. Saying the words out loud made the whole thing even more unbelievable.

"Sheriffs' departments all over the state seem to believe you shot them both."

"Me?"

He slapped something on the seat near her head.

She flinched, then looked to see what it was. A newspaper. The headline screamed Woman Wanted for Double Murder.

"You and your lover, this Davis guy, had a falling out when he refused to leave his wife. He broke it off between you during the hunting trip. So you shot him."

"That's not true! Mr. Davis was new to the company. I didn't know him beyond the office. I didn't shoot anyone!"

"They say Roger tried to stop you, so you shot him, too."

She shook her head. Jace couldn't believe that. Not after all they'd been through. Not after...

He pointed to the newspaper. "Read about it for yourself."

She moved her eyes over the newsprint, not really seeing the words. Below the fold, a photo of herself stared back at her. Her vision blurred. The black-and-white words of the story blended to a hazy gray. "If you believe I did what they say, if you believe I'm a murderer, why didn't you turn me in? There was a deputy right there. Why did you smuggle me out in this truck?"

"I wanted to ask you myself. I wanted to witness your reaction, see if you've been feeding me a load of bull."

She looked at him directly, unblinking. "Then look, dammit."

He glanced at her.

"I didn't shoot anyone. I don't know what happened on the ridge, not after I ran. But the last I saw, both Mr. Davis and your friend Roger were alive. I swear it."

He turned his eyes back to the highway. Lips pressed in a line, he drove, saying nothing.

Shanna's pulse pounded over the roar of the engine. Jace had to believe her. She'd just met the man yesterday, but over the past hours, she'd thought she felt something meld between them. Some kind of bond. What? Trust? She didn't know. But in less than an hour since they'd reached Copperville, it had all fallen apart.

Maybe they didn't really trust each other. Maybe he'd never trusted her. Maybe she just *wanted* to trust him.

Maybe she just wanted so badly to be able to trust *anyone.*

A minute stretched to five. The truck's floorboards grew hot. Her legs grew stiff. Still, she didn't dare move. She watched Jace's face, trying to guess what he'd do next.

Finally Jace glanced down at her. "You can get up now. No one will notice you out here."

She straightened her cramping legs and slid into the seat. She stretched the seat belt across her chest.

The Wyoming countryside whizzed past outside the window. Oil rigs protruded from the dry brown valley. Mountain peaks loomed to the front and driver's side, dusted white with snow. Judging from the slant of the evening sun, they were moving north. Back in the direction they came.

Shanna swallowed into a dry throat. "You're taking me back?"

Jace gave his head a shake. "I'm taking you to Palmer."

"Palmer?" To her apartment? To Emily? "What happened to going to the next county? What happened to getting someone impartial to investigate?"

"You're wanted for a double murder. You're the subject of a statewide manhunt. There's no such thing as impartiality anymore."

She nodded. "So I turn myself in. Prove myself innocent in court."

Jace let out a harsh laugh. "Charged with a double murder? With Barstow and the sheriff as witnesses against you? Sorry, Shanna, but you don't stand a chance."

He was right. If Mr. Barstow and the sheriff said they saw her shoot those men, there would be no jury in the state that would believe her.

She studied Jace's face. His jaw was still hard, still set, but she could swear there was something a little softer in his eyes. "Do *you* believe me?"

"That's not going to matter one way or the other."

"It matters to me."

He glanced at her.

There it was, that tenderness. The same light in his eyes that she'd seen in the mountains. She was sure of it. Almost sure. She needed to hear the words from his lips. "You do believe me, don't you?"

"I believe you."

Warmth flooded through her body. She might be in bad

trouble, but at least Jace believed in her. And knowing that gave her just enough hope to carry on. "So what can we do?"

"Find out why Barstow wanted you dead in the first place, then use it to prove you were set up."

She could see where he was leading. "And the only way to find that out is to look at the files I was working on, see what Barstow thinks I know."

"That's right."

Shanna settled into the passenger seat and set her sights on the road ahead. The miles whirred under the truck's tires just as thoughts whirred in her head. She knew she should be thinking about what she'd worked on in previous weeks, but all she could wrap her mind around was the ache in her arms, the longing in her chest, the need to hold her baby in her arms again.

She hadn't said a word to Jace about her daughter. Here she'd been suspicious of him for not sharing the details of his life when she hadn't trusted him with her own...especially her most precious detail of all. But now it looked like he might be the only person she *could* trust. "We need to make a short stop when we get to town."

He arched his brows in a silent question. "Not your apartment. The police will be watching it. That's the first place they'll expect you to go. That or the bus station."

"No, not my apartment. My friend Linda's place."

"This Linda, she works with you?"

"She's my best friend...and Mr. Barstow's assistant."

"And you think she knows something?"

"About the hunting trip? No. Linda thought Barstow inviting me along meant I was getting a promotion." She allowed herself a bitter smile. Anthony Barstow's world was very different from anything she or Linda had imagined, and so were his plans for Shanna. "But if I'm going to get into

Talbot to search the company's records, I'm going to need a security card to get into the building. And I don't think it would be a good idea to use the one with my name on it."

"Linda will give you hers?"

"Yes." At least she thought so. And while she was getting the card, she could give Emily what might be the last hug they would ever share.

Jace nodded. "Point the way."

HE HAD TO BE out of his mind.

Shifting on the truck's worn-out seat, Jace piloted the beater onto Palmer's aptly named Main Street, the main thoroughfare in town. He was driving straight into a bad situation, he knew that. A situation that might land him back behind bars. But he didn't know what else to do.

Or at least, what else he could live with.

It would be easier if he didn't buy Shanna's story. If he thought she was capable of aiming a rifle at a man and pulling the trigger. If he believed she had it in her to look him in the face and lie. But he didn't. And no amount of cooked-up evidence was going to convince him otherwise.

Walking away wasn't an option. Not anymore. Not for him. He couldn't leave Shanna to fend for herself, and he couldn't forget Roger. And he sure as hell couldn't let Barstow get away with buying and selling justice like he did uranium ore.

He glanced at Shanna. She'd been quiet since he'd grilled her, as if her thoughts were someplace else. Hopefully she was figuring out what it was that Barstow wanted to keep quiet. "Where does Linda live?"

"She bought one of the new condos down off of Country Club Road."

"Nice." Jace didn't know Palmer well, but he knew

Barstow's assistant must be making pretty good money to live in that area. He could still remember the locals moaning their worries about Palmer's transformation from cattle town to yuppieville, and their fears it would become a second Jackson Hole. But that was before the energy boom took hold. Now the old ranch culture was being overrun, not by national forest land and latte shops, but by oil derricks and strip mines.

Too bad.

Not that he had anything against men who worked in the oil fields and mines. But the men in charge, the ones with clean fingernails and filthy consciences like Barstow? They stank more than the oil derricks and were more poisonous than uranium waste.

Shanna pointed out a turn, and he took it. The groomed lawns of a golf course flanked one side of the road, fancy houses the other. It took about a blink to get to the Mountain View Condominiums. Palmer might be the most populated town in the county, but that didn't mean it was large. Large in Wyoming was reserved for mountains and sky.

Jace pulled to the side of the road around the corner from the address and switched off the engine. The truck clunked loudly as it died. It was amazing the two-hundred-dollar investment had gotten them so far. It would stand out in this neighborhood, but that couldn't be helped. His biggest worry was the police staking out Shanna's friend's condo. "We'll circle past her place first, make sure no one is waiting for us."

Shanna nodded.

"I know Linda's your friend, but let me talk to her. At least at first."

He was waiting for an argument, but Shanna just nodded again.

They climbed out of the truck and completed the circuitous trek before approaching the friend's door. There was no sign of surveillance. So far, so good. If he was in the lead, he could control the situation, focus on getting the security card and getting out. The less information they gave Linda about where they'd been and where they were going, the less she'd have to wrestle with telling the sheriff or deputies when they, inevitably, came to question her.

He let Shanna lead him to the right door and press the doorbell. Waiting for an answer, she glanced down the street. She raised to her toes, then bounced back down, flat-footed.

She seemed nervous, not that she didn't have reason. But Jace couldn't help but wonder if she was more concerned about her friend's support than she'd let on.

The porch light flashed on. The door jolted inward. A well-dressed, long-haired brunette stared with wide, brown eyes. "Shanna!"

"Linda, I'm so glad to see you."

"Shanna! What happened? What's going—" Shanna's friend's attention narrowed on Jace, as if suddenly realizing he was there. "Who the hell are you?"

"A friend." He glanced down the street. No sign of police, but he didn't like the noisy scene they were making at the door. A scene dramatic enough for neighbors to note. "Can we come in?"

"Come in?" she parroted. She turned back to Shanna without stepping aside. "What happened? On TV they're saying… horrible things."

"We'll explain inside." Jace pushed his way past Linda, pulling Shanna with him. He closed the door safely behind them.

"You wouldn't believe what I've been through, Lin." Shanna held out her arms to give her friend a hug.

Linda didn't respond. "I think I deserve an explanation." Jace stepped forward, placing himself between Shanna and her friend. "We need your help, Linda. Shanna needs your help. And for now, you're going to have to trust her."

"Mommy?"

Jace looked down, following the sound of the little voice.

A little girl with strawberry-blond hair and twinkling eyes darted around the brunette's legs and reached her little arms up to Shanna. "Mommy! You're back!"

# *Chapter Eight*

A jolt shot up Jace's spine. He watched Shanna scoop the girl up and hug her little body. She closed her eyes, petting the girl's hair. Teardrops wound down her cheeks.

*Shanna had a daughter?*

He shook his head. She'd never said a thing. Never even given him a hint there was a little girl tied up in this. A child to protect.

"The police are looking for you, Shanna." Linda's voice cut through Jace's jangled mind.

Shanna didn't open her eyes. She twisted at the waist, rocking her little girl back and forth.

"Did you hear me? They say you killed Ron Davis. They say you're dangerous. They say—"

"Hold on." Jace held up a hand to silence Linda. He had to get a hold on this situation. First thing was to get the security card and get out before a well-meaning neighbor made a call to the police. "We can't talk about this right now. We need your help."

Linda looked at him as if he'd just said the most outlandish thing she'd ever heard. "Help? I don't even know you."

"Shanna needs your help."

Linda shook her head, as if she still wasn't understanding what he was trying to say. "Shanna is wanted by the police."

Jace spoke slowly. He needed to calm her down. Make her think. He needed her to understand before panic swept her away. "It's all a mistake, Linda."

"They had her picture on CNN."

"Shanna didn't kill Ron Davis. She didn't kill Roger Harris."

Linda shook her head. "That's not what they said. It was on TV."

"They lied, Linda. Anthony Barstow killed those men."

She shook her head.

Damn. This was like talking to a boulder.

"Linda, Anthony Barstow tried to kill Shanna, too."

"Mommy?" The little girl's voice shrilled with panic. She clung to Shanna like a frightened kitten.

Damn. He didn't want to freak the little girl out, but he needed to make Shanna's friend understand.

"We need your help, Linda. We need your help finding the truth."

"The truth?" Linda shook her head again. She stepped back and reached for something on a table near the door.

A phone.

Jace grabbed her wrist before she could punch 9-1-1. "There's no need to call anyone. Just hear me out."

"Let me go."

He didn't want to hurt this woman, but he would before he let her make a phone call that would spin this mess totally out of his control.

As if he had control now.

"It's okay, Linda," Shanna said.

"Shanna." Her friend looked from Jace's hand to Shanna and back again.

"Please, Linda. I didn't do it. You have to believe me."

Linda looked confused. She looked as if she was about to cry. "You're hurting me."

Jace loosened his grip, but he didn't let go. He could see now that Linda wasn't about to listen to anything he said, let alone hand over a security card. Hell, he was probably lucky the phone wasn't a gun.

He glanced at Shanna.

The little girl had pulled away from Shanna's neck and was looking at him, a pensive pucker to her mouth.

A new jolt of surprise went through him. A daughter. Shanna had a daughter. Why hadn't she told him? What the hell was he going to do now?

Shanna took a step toward her friend. "Please, Linda. I'll explain everything. Then if you still want to call the police, you're more than welcome."

Linda hesitated. Ten seconds. Twenty. She released the phone.

Jace let out a tense breath. He stuffed the telephone in his coat pocket.

Shanna set her daughter down. The girl wrapped her little arms around her mother's legs and clung. Shanna stroked the girl's hair, focusing on her friend. "I don't know what they told you, Linda, but I didn't do anything."

"The police came by Talbot earlier. The police and the sheriff. They said…" Linda glanced at the girl. "They said you're guilty of homicide. *Intentional* homicide."

At least Linda was thinking now, aware of what she was saying in front of the little girl. Jace would take that as a good sign.

Shanna shook her head. "It wasn't like that. Not at all. I didn't do anything like that."

"Then why would they say it?"

"I'll tell you everything. Explain everything." Shanna raised her eyes to Jace. "Could you play with Emily for a second?"

Jace paused. Telling Linda everything was a bad idea. Even though Shanna had convinced her to turn over the phone, the woman still seemed so confused and frightened, he wasn't sure what she'd do. The more they told her, the more he feared would get back to the Palmer police...back to the county sheriff.

Not only that, but Jace had no idea what to do with the little girl. Not that he disliked children. Not at all. But from what he remembered about Darla's kids, little Emily's questions promised to be more probing than Linda's.

"Please?" She gestured into the heart of a spacious great room where a television played a cartoon about a red dog. "She can watch Clifford. It'll give me a chance to explain the situation to Linda."

"Explain the situation?" Jace gave her a warning look he hoped she could read.

She shot her own pointed look back. "Yes. I need Linda to understand what happened. All of it. I'll just be a few minutes."

"Right." A few minutes, provided Linda swallowed the wild tale a lot more readily than she had so far. Not that he could blame her. God knew, he'd had his own problems with that.

A tug on his coat brought his attention back to the little girl. Wide green eyes turned on him. Tear tracks still glistened wet on her cheeks, but she no longer looked afraid. Mommy was making things better, he supposed. That's how Emily would see it.

If only it were that easy.

"I have Power Rangers," she said.

He wasn't sure what to say. "Really?"

"Yeah. They're super cool."

Jace almost groaned. Seeing those cute, vulnerable little eyes staring up at him was more than he could take. He stepped farther into the condo. The television. He'd make for the television. "Why don't you watch your show? See? The red dog is doing something over there."

"I have a red Power Ranger you can play with. He's a boy."

"I see." He pointed again at the cartoon. "Clifford is red."

"I have the pink Ranger and the yellow Ranger, too. But they're girls."

What a joke. He'd meant to control this situation, and at the moment he couldn't even control a child probably too young to go to kindergarten.

He made one last-ditch effort. "What about the TV?"

"You can play with the yellow one if you want to." She handed him the little yellow-suited plastic woman, though judging from her pout, the offer was a major sacrifice.

He let out a long breath. "I'll take the red one."

Pink lips curved into a wide smile. She scampered away. A moment later she was back, thrusting a red-suited man toward him. "He's the leader."

Jace took the toy. He vaguely remembered a variety of Power Rangers television shows from years ago. They must be replaying the series on cable. Or maybe they were making new ones, for all he knew.

He studied the little red man. "The leader, huh?" With Emily playing with the two female Rangers, Jace doubted the red guy was anything but a figurehead.

"Yeah. The Rangers fight bad guys and help people. He's the best fighter of all."

"That's cool."

"He can fight all the bad guys. He can keep them from hurting Mommy."

So much for keeping the details from the little girl.

"He can, can't he?" she asked. "He can help Mommy? He can keep her safe?"

Looking into that tender face, there was only one answer he could give. "Yes. He can."

She beamed at Jace as if he himself was the red Ranger.

Man, was he in trouble.

Tearing his eyes from the little girl, he found Shanna. She was still in the front hall with Linda, her hands splayed out in front of her, pleading her case to her friend in a hushed voice.

Linda's face pinched with concern.

Maybe Shanna was getting somewhere. Maybe pawning off Emily on him had done more than prevent tender ears from hearing more about Shanna's ordeal. Maybe Linda was more open to her friend without a strange man hanging around.

Headlights prismed in the leaded-glass sidelights flanking the front door.

A car.

Adrenaline spiked his pulse. "Shanna?"

Shanna followed his gaze to the window. She gasped. "The police."

## Chapter Nine

Shanna peered through the sidelight flanking Linda's front door. A black-and-white Palmer cruiser came to a stop behind the beater truck, its lights shining on the license plate.

Good. It would take a few moments to call in the plate and find out who owned it before the cop came to the door. With any luck, and some help, she and Jace would be long gone. She grasped Linda's hands. "I need your help."

Linda tore her eyes from the window and shook her head. "I can't lie to the police."

"Then don't lie. Just stall them. Long enough for us to get away. Can you do that?"

"I don't know."

Maybe she was asking her friend too much. Linda had grown up with a tough family life. From what she'd told Shanna, the sheriff had often come to her house to break up fights before her father had finally died while driving drunk. Shanna bringing this kind of thing back into Linda's life was traumatic for her friend. "I'm so sorry to do this to you, Linda. You've got to believe me, if there was any other way…"

Linda shook her head as if breaking herself from a trance. "There is a way. Turn yourself in."

"I can't do that. Not yet."

"Why not? What good does running do, Shanna? Are you going to run all your life?" Linda looked past Shanna. Her mouth shifted into a worried line.

Shanna knew she was looking at Em, but she couldn't follow her friend's gaze. Even thinking about leaving her daughter again made her sinuses burn with tears. "I have to find out why Mr. Barstow wanted me dead. I have to get some kind of evidence. They won't believe me otherwise. No one will."

Linda glanced out the window.

Shanna was afraid to look. Afraid to see if the officer had gotten out of the car. Afraid to see how close he was to the door. "Please, Linda."

"I'll stall them. But I can't lie. I don't want to go to jail."

"No. None of us wants you to go to jail, Linda." Least of all Shanna. Not only was Linda her best friend, she was the only person she'd trust with Emily. If Linda wasn't able to take care of Em, Shanna didn't know what she'd do.

But that wasn't the end of the favors she needed from Linda. Shanna flinched at the thought of asking. If she had another alternative, she wouldn't. But as things were, she couldn't think of one. "There's something else."

"What?"

"Your security card."

"My security card?" Linda frowned. "For the office?"

"I need to borrow it. And your number."

"Why?"

"The evidence I need. Finding out why Mr. Barstow wants me dead is my only chance to clear my name."

Linda nodded, as if the situation was finally sinking in. She started for the kitchen, motioning for Shanna to follow.

Shanna shot Jace a look, then went after Linda. Jace and Emily met them in the kitchen.

Linda rummaged through her purse and pulled out a piece

of plastic the size of a credit card. She handed it to Shanna. "Four-four-six-two."

Shanna stuffed the card into her coat pocket and repeated the number, committing it to memory. "Thank you, Linda. You're the best."

"Don't you forget it." Linda pulled back and gave her a sad smile. "Where are you going? Where are you going to stay?"

"We don't know." Jace pulled Linda's phone from his coat and set it on the kitchen table. "You probably don't want to have to lie about that anyway."

Linda nodded. "Right."

The doorbell chime echoed through the condo.

Linda gestured to the sliding-glass door behind the dinette. "Go. I'll stall them." She left the kitchen.

Shanna knelt down to Em. Tears clogged her throat and made her head throb. "You be a good girl for Linda, okay, Emily?"

"You can't go, Mommy."

"I have to, sweetie. But I'll be back as soon as I can."

"Can I go, too?"

"No, baby. You need to stay here with Linda."

"But I want to stay with you."

"I know you do. And I want to stay with you, too. But I have to go for a little while longer."

"And then you'll come back?"

A shudder racked Shanna's shoulders, as a sob tried to break loose. She struggled to force it back.

"You'll come back, won't you, Mommy?"

"Yes, sweetheart. I'll come back." She pulled her daughter close again, the last of her words muffled in the child's hair.

Jace slid the glass door open. "We have to go, Shanna."

She forced her arms to let Emily go and stood. "I'll miss you, baby."

Tears spiked Emily's eyelashes. "Mommy. Don't go."

Shanna's head whirled. How could she walk out that door? How could she leave when every cell in her body screamed for her to stay? To wrap her arms around her little girl and never let go?

Jace bent down and fitted his palm over Em's little blond head. His hand totally covered her skull like a cap. "Don't worry, Emily. Your mom will come back. Everything will be okay."

"You promise?"

"Of course. I'm the red Ranger, aren't I?"

"Yes," she whispered. She held out her red Power Ranger toy and pushed it into Jace's hand.

Jace took it from her and stuffed it in his pocket. "Then you don't have to worry." He closed his hand around Shanna's arm and pulled her out the door.

Shanna watched fat tears roll down Emily's face as Jace slid the door closed behind her. She raised a hand and forced herself to smile, for Emily's sake. "Bye-bye, sweetheart." Then she turned away and followed Jace into the darkness without looking back.

SHANNA STOOD AT the edge of the new Wal-Mart's parking lot and watched the road for any sign of Palmer police or county sheriff's cars. From the look of things, Linda had been able to stall them long enough that they couldn't figure out where she and Jace had gone.

So far, so good.

Jace had ventured inside the store while she waited on the edge of the parking lot. She couldn't risk being caught by a security camera or recognized by the greeter. By the time he returned, laden down with three bags of supplies, she was so cold, she couldn't stop shaking. "What next?"

He reached into one of the bags and pulled out a strip of beef jerky. He stripped the plastic off one and handed it to Shanna.

She bit into it, unable to chew and swallow it fast enough.

Jace unwrapped a second stick for himself. "We need wheels."

She nodded. They'd had to leave the junker truck he'd bought in Copperville outside Linda's place. With the police car parked behind it, they didn't dare try to circle back. "Any ideas?"

He scanned the lot, as if expecting to find a convenient vehicle boasting a For Sale sign. Or maybe this time he was contemplating stealing something.

The pit of her stomach hollowed out. She'd been a law-abiding citizen her whole life, never mind that she was now accused of murder. The idea of actually being guilty of something nauseated her.

And of course, she couldn't shake the thought that Jace had actually done time in jail.

"We also need a place to stay," said Jace, "at least for the night."

A place to sleep, maybe even to shower. The thought made her mouth water as much as the beef jerky she was devouring. "A motel?"

"The police and sheriff will be looking at the motels around here. Especially once they know we were at your friend Linda's."

She thought about the scene at Linda's. Her friend's shock and fear. Emily's tears. The toy she'd given Jace and the promise he'd given in return. "Thank you for being so good to Emily."

Jace pressed his lips in a grim line. He looked hard, like

he had when he'd found her in his garage, when he'd grilled her in the truck. "You didn't tell me you had a daughter."

"I should have. I know." She'd known he'd be upset that she hadn't told him everything. She could tell from the moment he'd seen Emily. But Emily hadn't had anything to do with Talbot or Mr. Barstow or any of this nightmare. She didn't see how he had the right to be angry that she hadn't told him about her daughter. "I needed to protect her. Until I knew more about you."

She expected his expression to soften. It didn't. If anything, his eyes felt as if they were drilling into her. "You should have told me. Before I brought you back to Palmer."

"Why?"

"She makes things a lot more complicated."

She wasn't following. "How? She's just a little girl. She has nothing to do with any of this."

"That's where you're wrong." A muscle clenched along his jaw. He peered out over the parking lot. "Here we go. Our ride."

She followed his narrowed gaze, grateful not to be under those hard eyes, yet uneasy that she still didn't understand what he was getting at.

A pickup hooked to a fifth wheel drove into the parking lot. It stopped in the back of the lot and three men climbed out.

Shanna glanced back at Jace. "You're not going to—"

He gave her a frown. "What? Steal their rig? No. We're going to stow away."

Heat tinged her cheeks. Great. He probably figured that now that she knew he'd done time, she was waiting for him to break the law any moment. "How do you know where they're heading?"

"I don't. Not exactly. But I can tell you that they're on their way out of town."

"How do you know that?"

"Their clothes are too clean for them to be returning from a hunting trip."

Shanna watched the men walk toward the store. Jace was right. They wore pants similar to her insulated ones. The only difference was theirs looked almost new. She was a wrinkled, dirty mess.

Though she was sure being prey was a dirtier business than the role of hunter.

As the men disappeared into the store, Jace strode toward their camper. "We'll let them drive us to the outskirts of town, someplace there might be some vacant vacation cabins or trailers. I figure you can tell me when we need to jump out."

Jumping out of a camper didn't sound like fun. But then walking more miles didn't appeal, either. Sleep. That's what she needed. And a shower. Maybe then she could soak in what Jace was talking about. Maybe then she could make sense of it.

She watched as Jace pulled a screwdriver from his bag of purchases and fitted it under the door's handle. He wrenched it to the side, using leverage to pit screwdriver against lock.

The lock lost.

Definitely criminal. But then, since she was already wanted by the police, maybe she should get used to it. Maybe she should start rethinking a few things.

She slipped into the camper, Jace behind her. It was dark inside, but her eyes soon adjusted to the parking-lot lights squeaking through the slits in the window blinds.

Jace placed a hand on each of her arms and steered her down a pinched hall.

She stumbled up a few stairs. Hunching under the low

ceiling, she slid open a curtain. A bed filled the small room, stretching almost the width of the camper. She looked to the left and right, but an assortment of suitcases and bags left little space to walk around the bed.

"Just climb on top." Crouching low, Jace offered her a hand. "We'll hide in here. In case they load their supplies in the trailer."

His logic made perfect sense. Still, logic or no, a shimmer worked its way through her chest as she took his hand and climbed on the bed. Jace slid the curtain closed before sinking onto the mattress next to her.

Silence hung between them, thick and intimate as it had in the wilderness. Shanna bit her lip to keep herself from filling the void with words. There was no telling when the owners of the fifth wheel would return. The last thing she wanted to do was be caught yapping and give them away.

The sound of male voices rumbled outside. Doors slammed. An engine roared. The camper lurched into motion. Bands of light and dark moved over the bed, then faded to black as the camper left town and started its ascent toward the mountains.

Shanna's urge to speak faded. The silence still felt intimate, loaded in a way speech never did. But as their bodies swayed together on the bed, it somehow started feeling more normal. Minutes ticked away, one after the next. If she figured correctly, they were heading up along the river. They should be reaching the campground soon. She nodded to Jace.

He must have caught her movement even in the dark, because he climbed off the bed. Again offering his hand, he helped her up and they descended the steps to the door.

Shanna gripped the rail flanking the inside of the door and peered out the tiny window. Lights from Palmer sparkled behind them. To the left, the dark peaks of mountains rimmed the horizon. That put them somewhere in the winding foot-hills west of town. Her hunch was right. They passed what looked like the roof peaks of several cabins. The small camp-ground scrolled past.

She turned to Jace, unable to see anything but his silhouette inside the dark camper. "This is as good an area as any."

"All right." Jace gripped the door handle and raised his brows in her direction. "Ready?"

She guessed she was as ready as she ever would be. She nodded.

The van slowed further. Jace pushed open the door. Air rushed through, making a howling sound. Shanna could see mountain peaks rising in the distance. He shoved one of the plastic bags out the door. Top tied, the bag bounced and rolled into the ditch. He followed with the other. Jace turned to her and nodded. "We aren't going fast, but it's going to hurt all the same."

"Thanks for the warning." As if her neck and leg and every other muscle in her body didn't hurt enough already. She grasped the doorjamb and pulled herself to the threshold. Gravel and scrub brush whizzed by below her feet. Her mus-cles clamped down. Her pulse pounded in her ears. About the last thing she wanted to do was throw herself out of a moving camper.

"Keep your knees bent. You can do it."

A surge rippled through her at the confident tone of his voice. She scooped in a deep breath and jumped.

The first impact shuddered through her feet and up her legs. She toppled forward in a somersault, flipping and scuffing through the gravel. Finally she stopped, sprawled on her knees, her throat filled with dust and the scent of sagebrush.

Farther up the road, Jace threw himself out of the camper

and rolled, his exit looking much more controlled than Shanna's had felt.

She pushed to her bruised knees and brushed her hands along her thighs. Pain burned raw from her palms. Her sore neck and bruised leg screamed. At least those injuries would heal. Unlike broken bones. Or a bullet to the head.

The camper hesitated at the corner stop sign and kept going, as if unaware they had passengers.

She was on her feet by the time Jace joined her. She motioned back in the direction they had come. "I think I saw a couple of cabins back before the campground. This time of year, at least one has to be vacant, right?"

"We might have our pick."

Shanna pulled her coat tighter around her shoulders and they started walking. Jace picked up two of the bags of supplies and she grabbed one. She tried her best not to limp. As they circled the bend in the road, the trees opened up. The lights of Palmer sparkled below, like a cluster of stars. "We're still pretty close."

"Close enough to be able to get back and forth."

"It's still a long walk." For a moment, she actually wished Jace had stolen a car from the parking lot.

"Maybe we'll get lucky."

"And find a car with the keys inside just waiting for our use?"

"Or an ATV. I saw paths running parallel to the road that had to be made by some kind of sporting vehicle."

"Okay. I'm crossing my fingers for an ATV."

Sure enough, the next bend in the road was flanked by dirt ruts that could only have come from some kind of off-road vehicle. A half mile down the mountain, they ran into a cabin. Two three-wheeled ATVs sat in the gravel drive. Smoke poured from the chimney.

"So what now? Do we steal them?" She couldn't believe the words were coming from her mouth…and that she didn't feel more guilt in saying them.

Jace shook his head. "We don't want to draw attention to ourselves if we don't have to. We keep walking."

They continued down the road. The rugged landscape seemed more sinister in the dark than it had under the unrelenting sun. Every bend in the road or copse of evergreen set her nerves on edge. As if she was waiting for Mr. Barstow to jump out at any second, rifle pointed at her head.

At least the previous night, hunkered down with Jace in the mountains, the world had seemed big…too big for Mr. Barstow and the sheriff to ever find her. Now she felt like a girl at a small high school, bound to run into the class bully at any moment. And the fact that Palmer was her home and a place she'd once felt safe gave her the unsettling sensation that she'd never be safe again.

"There."

She followed Jace's gesture. Nestled between rock and tree sat a cabin. A house, really. The windows stared at them like black eyes. Shanna tried not to shiver. At least it appeared vacant. "Pretty fancy for a cabin."

Jace grunted. "Fancier than my house."

Her apartment, too. They walked to a door in the side of the garage. "You don't think the owners just use this for a vacation cabin, do you?"

"There's no dead bolt, so let's find out." Jace stepped back from the door. He raised his leg and kicked right below the knob, throwing his weight into the effort. The lock popped and the door snapped open.

Shanna held her breath and followed Jace inside. The garage was empty, no cars. It was likely their impression from the outside was right. No one home. She let the breath she'd been holding stream through her lips. Now, if it could just stay that way.

"Would you look at this."

She turned to see Jace bending over a couple of bikes. "Motorcycles?"

He stepped to the side. "Dirt bikes. But it will do for getting back into town."

He moved on to the inside door. Unlocked, the knob twisted easily under his hand.

They entered a cozy kitchen with butcher-block countertops. Yellow curtains framed the windows and yellow rugs lay scattered on the rich hardwood floor. If Shanna didn't feel so paranoid, she might even call it homey.

Of course she supposed she wasn't being paranoid if people actually *were* out to get her. "How do you know someone isn't going to be home? Someone could drive in any minute."

"I don't think so."

"How do you know?"

Jace tapped the thermostat just inside the door to the garage. "The heat is turned down."

She'd gotten so used to the cold over the past two days, she hadn't even noticed that the cabin was only a little warmer inside than a refrigerator. Of course, she was still bundled in her filthy hunting garb. "Were you able to find some clothing?" She nodded to the bags. She hadn't even thought to ask when he'd emerged from the store.

Jace strode into the kitchen. After dialing the thermostat to a livable temperature, he plunked the plastic bags he was carrying on the countertop. "I bought you many gifts."

She set her bag down and shrugged out of her heavy hunting parka. "What kind of gifts?"

He reached into the bag and pulled out a pair of jeans, a button-down shirt and a jacket that looked like shearling. He tossed her a bottle of shampoo and a T-shirt styled night-gown.

"Oh, my gosh. These are fantastic."

"That's not all." He dipped his hand in once more. This time he handed her scissors and a small box. Hair color. "A whole new you."

Reflexively, she raised her hand to her hair.

"Your picture is going to be all over the state."

She dropped her hand and nodded. He was right. There was no way she could stay in Palmer when her photo was all over the news. "Okay. Chop it off."

He picked up the scissors. "Ready?"

She wasn't the same woman she was before this all began. Somehow it seemed fitting that she didn't look the same. She picked up the box of hair color and studied it. Dark mahogany. It seemed to fit. Someone very different from her had hair the color of dark mahogany. Someone strong.

Someone who wasn't prey. "I've never been so ready in my life."

# *Chapter Ten*

"How do I look?"

Jace looked up into eyes that had become as familiar as his own in the last two days. But even though he'd cut Shanna's hair pixie-short himself and picked out the color at the store, seeing her was a shock.

Her eyes seemed impossibly big, her cheekbones as high as a model's, as if stripping away her clouds of luxuriously feminine hair had only served to emphasize just how feminine and beautiful her features were all on their own. The color of the nightgown echoed the pink flush the hot shower had brought to her cheeks.

"Well?"

He set down the sandwich he'd been eating. "You look great." His voice sounded husky, suggestive, not at all like he'd intended.

"You think people will recognize me?"

"If they look closely," he admitted.

She pursed her lips together in one of the sexiest looks he'd ever seen. "What else can I do? Sunglasses? Maybe a hat?"

He grabbed a pair of sunglasses from the bag he'd been emptying and flipped them to her. "Try these."

She slipped them on. "Better?"

He handed her a tube of lipstick he'd bought to complete her disguise.

"Red lipstick? I've never worn red lipstick." She opened the package and applied it. She pursed her lips again like a movie star blowing a kiss. "Now, this is cool."

She was going to kill him yet. She had to be tired, didn't she? He sure was. But right about now his body seemed anything but tired. "The good thing is that most people don't look closely at anything. Of course, the way you look, they probably won't want to take their eyes off you."

He forced his gaze back to the television screen. Maybe he should just keep his damn mouth shut. It was bad enough that he felt this attracted to Shanna. He sure didn't need to let her know it. Things were complicated enough already. "We need to figure out a game plan."

She circled the love seat and perched on the edge next to him. She slipped off the sunglasses. Unfortunately that left him with an unobstructed view of her eyes. "We should go early, before anyone but the security guard is in the building."

"We'll take the dirt bikes at dawn. What do you need to do to get through security?"

"With Linda's card and number, I should be able to slip both of us in undetected. The guard will be in the lobby. We'll go in the side entrance."

He could smell the soft scent of the shampoo she'd used. Floral, but with a sexy edge that made him want to breathe deeper. "Do they have cameras in the entrances or outside?"

"They do in the lobby. Also in the card scanner, but I think I can avoid it."

He wished she wouldn't look at him. "So it's settled. We'll go to Talbot early."

"Good." She didn't move from her perch.

Despite his better judgment, he allowed himself one more

peek. He hadn't been involved with a woman for a long time. But if he ever were to test those particular waters again, he could see testing them with a woman like Shanna. Tough and smart. A woman who could get bitten by a dog, hike through snowstorms and jump out of moving vehicles without one complaint.

And then turn around and make sense out of the financial records of a uranium mining company.

Too bad things weren't different.

She held his gaze for an uncomfortably long time. "I'm sorry I didn't tell you about Em."

His gut hitched. He hadn't been happy with that little surprise. Not that her daughter wasn't sweet as hell. But in this situation, she presented a problem. One he could easily see destroying all their best-laid plans. "I understand why you didn't."

"You could have fooled me."

"What?"

She paused, as if searching for the right words. "You seemed upset about Em at the parking lot, even angry."

He tilted his head to the side. He didn't want to talk about this. He wasn't sure what he felt about Emily and Shanna and this whole mess. He sure as hell didn't want to try to explain something he didn't fully understand himself. "Better get some sleep."

She nodded, but didn't move from her chair. "You said Em made things more complicated. How?"

He let out a sigh. If he made it simple, if he omitted the gray areas, the emotions involved, maybe he could help her see where he was coming from. "If Barstow can get to your daughter, he can get to you."

Her eyes flew wide. "You don't think he'd…" She covered her mouth with her fingers.

"I think he'd do whatever he needed to."

She jumped up from the love seat's arm as if ready to storm right back to that condo and lay her life down to protect her daughter.

He was sure she would, if given the chance. That's where the problem came in. He stood and grabbed her arm, right above the wrist. "Sit down."

"You just said—"

"I know what I just said." He almost groaned. He'd known how she would react, so why had he said it? Why hadn't he just kept his mouth shut? "Let me explain."

She didn't move.

"Come on." He guided her to sit beside him.

She perched on the edge of the cushion and watched him with wary eyes.

"Barstow doesn't have to do anything rash." Of course, that didn't mean he wouldn't, but Jace wouldn't mention that to Shanna. She already feared the worst. "He's a wealthy man. If he can buy off the sheriff, he can buy off child services."

"You think he'll try to take Emily away from me?"

"I'm saying it's a possibility. Your daughter makes you vulnerable."

She shook her head, as if she didn't want to accept it.

He moved his hand down her arm and laid it on top of hers. Maybe that's why he told her. Subconsciously he'd wanted to frighten her so he could provide comfort? Or had he wanted to push her away? Or maybe he just needed to get his worries out in the open…the worry that had hit him over the head when he'd seen her little girl. "It happened to a friend of mine. A lifetime ago."

"Mr. Barstow tried to take her child?"

"Not Barstow. Someone who runs in the same circles as Barstow. Duncan Masters. Big energy, big money."

She frowned. "Who was this woman? How do you know she didn't deserve to have her kid taken away? How do you know what really happened?"

"She was my partner."

"You lived together?"

He shook his head, though Darla had once been his partner in every other way, despite the warnings in department policy. "She was my partner. I was a cop. A detective."

"A cop?" Slowly her expression changed from confusion to understanding. "But you said you were in jail."

"It's a long story."

"We have time."

"Sure, if you're not interested in sleep."

He'd thrown in the comment for levity, but she didn't smile. "I've been straight with you. I've told you everything, even the stuff about Kurt. Things I haven't even told Linda. I think it's time you're straight with me."

"You're probably right." There was no point in hiding any of it anymore. If Shanna wanted to hurt him, she already had plenty of ammunition. And if she was aware of the dangers she faced, maybe she would be more prepared than Darla had been.

Even though he had no idea how anyone could be prepared for what his partner had faced.

He braced one elbow on the love seat's arm. The question was, how in the hell did he start?

Shanna watched him through narrowed eyes. "That explains a lot, you being a cop. Like the way you grilled me."

"Sorry I was so hard on you, but I needed to know you were telling the truth. All of it." Too bad he didn't realize she was still holding back until he saw that chubby-cheeked little face.

Shanna nodded, seemingly accepting his version of an

apology. "So this Duncan Masters, he tried to take your partner's kids away. Why?"

"We had a strong case against him."

"What did he do?"

"You seem to be pretty good at grilling people, too, when you want to be."

She didn't smile. "Answer the question."

"If you believe Masters, he didn't do a thing. The body in his swimming pool said different."

"He killed somebody?"

He hadn't talked about Duncan Masters for years. But even so, he could feel the heat rising in his blood. "His mistress. She also happened to work for him. And if you believe the e-mail they exchanged, she was tired of giving him the milk for free. She wanted him to leave his wife."

"So that's why you thought I was having an affair with Barstow."

"Love gone bad is always a strong motive for murder."

"What does this have to do with your partner's child?"

"Children. Two girls and a boy. Before we could get an arrest warrant, she got a visit from child services. They cited evidence of abuse. Got a child psychologist to swear to it."

"And you think Duncan Masters had something to do with it?"

"I don't think. I know. People like Masters and Barstow, they can buy anything they want. People, justice. Anything."

"You sound bitter."

"I am bitter." Dammit, he'd believed in justice. Not just as a political slogan or a quaint ideal, he'd believed it was real. He'd believed it was blind. He'd believed it was equal.

He'd been so damn stupid.

"So what happened? What did your partner do?"

He paused a long while, deciding what to reveal. "She

gave in. Gave him what he wanted. A walk on the murder charge."

"How?"

"By swearing that I falsified evidence to get the search warrant for Masters's house and the e-mails."

"But you didn't...."

"No. But it didn't matter. The evidence was thrown out. Masters beat the system. He proved he was above the law."

"What happened to you?"

"I was fired and brought up on charges."

"And that's how you ended up doing time in jail?"

"I was made to serve as an example for any cops who thought they were above the law." What a joke. That was when he knew the law was broken. That it only applied to people who didn't have millions in their bank accounts.

Why had he ever thought he could change that?

He met Shanna's eyes. Her beautiful green eyes. When he'd heard about Barstow hunting her down, he hadn't believed he could change things. Not really. But when he'd looked into her eyes, he'd wanted to try.

"You must hate her for it."

He snapped his attention to her words. "Hate who?"

"Your partner."

"Why? She couldn't have done anything different. She lived for those kids. If I had kids, I probably would have done the same."

"No, you wouldn't. You'd fight it out."

As much as he liked kids, as much as he'd thought he'd wanted them at one time, he didn't know what it was like to actually be a parent. However, he did remember the desperation in Darla's and Shanna's eyes when they believed their children were in danger. He'd seen what that desperation could make a person do. "I don't know."

"You're worried the same thing is going to happen with me and Em, aren't you? That if Mr. Barstow takes her away, I'll do whatever he wants."

He clenched his jaw. What could he say? It had also occurred to him that they'd need a fall guy. Someone to take the blame for Roger's and that Davis guy's deaths. Maybe someone with a ranch nearby, someone with a record and without an alibi. Maybe he was being paranoid, he didn't know. But he couldn't seem to shake it. Not totally.

He made a show of looking at his watch, even though his mind didn't register the time. "I've scraped at my bad memories and failures enough for one night. We'd better get some sleep. Dawn is going to come awfully fast."

She watched him, her eyes focused, sharp as shards of glass. "You don't just think I'll cave in. You're afraid I'll sell you out."

"What do you want me to say?"

She sat down on the love seat. For a moment her hand hovered near his knee, as if she wanted to touch him, but wasn't sure that she should. "I have to be honest. If he tries to have my baby taken away, I don't know what I'll do. But I won't sell you out, Jace."

"You can't say that."

"Yes. I can."

"Shanna, I know you feel grateful to me, even obligated, but that's not enough."

She withdrew her hand, clenching it into a fist in her lap. "You don't know what I feel. You don't know me at all. I won't sell you out."

Suddenly he was so tired it was all he could do to shake his head. "Shanna, everyone will sell another person out if the stakes are high enough."

DAWN CAME WAY TOO EARLY. As Shanna piloted the dirt bike into Palmer, its little motor buzzing in her ears, she ran over the conversation with Jace the night before. She couldn't argue that she wouldn't do anything to protect Em, but he'd been wrong about the rest. She wasn't like his ex-partner. She wouldn't sell him out. Not after all he'd done for her. Not after he'd saved her life. Not after…

She clamped her teeth to keep them from clattering together with the vibration of the bike. After Kurt had left, she swore she wouldn't get involved with a man again. She certainly wouldn't trust one with her heart. And although she wasn't willing to trust Jace in that way, she had to admit he made her want to. He made her want to take a chance.

Buzzing into town, she pushed all those "coulda, woulda, shoulda" thoughts to the back of her mind. She couldn't afford to think about what would never be. She needed to focus on what was. And right now that meant figuring out why her boss wanted her dead.

The streets were quiet. Few people were up and around yet, besides truckloads of workers heading for nearby oil fields and mines to start their days. Already the summer's tourist traffic had cleared out. Except for a small infusion of hunters, only local residents stuck around this time of year. Soon winter would slow Palmer to a crawl. Particularly in the off-season, the local economy ran on big energy. And in Palmer, that primarily meant Talbot Mining.

She turned the corner off Main Street before they reached the Talbot building and led Jace to the alley behind a video-rental place. After they'd lost the beater truck outside Linda's, she and Jace had planned to park even farther away from their destination this time. That way, if something went wrong, they could still double back and get the motorbikes.

She turned off the dirt bike's ignition and climbed off. Up

ahead near the Talbot building, a small group of people milled on the sidewalk flanking Main. "That's strange. I wonder what's going on."

Jace swung a leg off his dirt bike and stashed it behind the building, leaning it against the whitewashed concrete wall. "Is there a tour or something scheduled?"

"Talbot doesn't give tours of its headquarters. Not that there's much to see. It's just an office building." Shanna hid her bike, as well. She pulled off her gloves and rubbed her hands together, trying to erase the vibration from the bike's shrill little motor while she combed the faces of the small crowd. She didn't recognize anyone. Dressed in heavy coats, mittens, hats and scarves, they looked like they planned to spend the day outside.

Jace jerked his head back. "I know what it is. The mill."

"The mill?"

"The uranium mill in the Red Desert Basin. The one Talbot is trying to reopen. There's a protest scheduled for this morning. I saw it mentioned on the news back in Copperville."

The Red Desert Basin mill had been shut down long before Shanna came to the company, after the scares at Three Mile Island and Chernobyl had made people wary of nuclear power. But in the past few years, world demand for uranium had grown. And once again, Wyoming uranium mines and milling capacity were on the upswing. "I worked on the profit projections for reopening that mill."

"Notice anything unusual?"

"Not unless the promise of significant profits is unusual. Reopening the mill is going to be a boon to Talbot and the whole Red Desert Basin." She gestured to the small crowd of people. "Don't tell me. An environmental group?"

He nodded.

That made sense. Increased uranium production brought

increased waste materials and fears of contamination. Fears that weren't totally unfounded. Shanna could understand the ambitions and worries of both sides.

"What if Barstow thinks you know something that would keep the mill from opening?"

"Like what?"

"I don't know, safety concerns? Something you could feed to a group like this?"

She shook her head. "If that's what he's trying to cover up, he should have invited the project manager on his little hunting trip. I deal with numbers. I don't have any more information about the actual mining or refining operations than your average citizen on the street."

Jace started walking toward Main Street and the Talbot building. "Any ideas how we're going to get past this group without being spotted?"

"Luck."

He gestured to the building with the sweep of an arm. "Lead the way."

She tore her gaze from the protestors and started across the street. Housed in a square, three-story stone building, Talbot had always looked to Shanna as if it had emerged straight out of the old west, even though she knew the building had actually been built during the 1980s energy boom. Today her view of the solid and imposing structure was far less romantic. Today the way the morning sun reflected off stone and glass just gave her the creeps.

"Excuse me, do you work here?"

She whirled around at the voice.

A tanned man with high cheekbones and long hair pulled back in a severe ponytail walked toward them.

One of the protestors? Or someone who recognized her from the pictures on the news? "Who are you?"

"Boyd Davidson." He caught up to them, but didn't offer his hand. "I'm president of Citizens of the Earth."

So much for luck.

"The activist group protesting the mill," Jace added.

Davidson gave him a sideways look. "The mill poses a threat to our groundwater. The first year of waste alone will make the area around the mill uninhabitable."

Shanna shook her head. She didn't want to get into a debate with this guy, but his facts were not entirely accurate. "The waste material is a problem only if it's not disposed of properly. Talbot—"

"Do you really think a corporation as big as Talbot gives a damn how they dispose of the waste? The only thing that matters to them is money."

Shanna held up a hand. What was she thinking? She shouldn't have said anything. She didn't want to argue with Mr. Davidson. She didn't want to be noticed at all. And she certainly didn't want to do anything that would cause people to remember her. "You're right."

Davidson looked at her from under lowered brows. "We need to talk to Anthony Barstow, and we're not leaving here until we do."

Fine with her. In fact, the busier Boyd Davidson kept Mr. Barstow, the better. "Good luck with that." Shanna stepped around him and made for the side entrance.

"Wait," Davidson boomed. "I want you to tell him that. Tell him I'm waiting out here for him. Tell him he doesn't have the right to run roughshod over the people and wildlife who live in the Red Desert Basin."

"You can tell him when he arrives. He drives a black SUV with a personalized plate. You can't miss him."

"We aren't leaving until our concerns are heard," Davidson

shouted, more for the benefit of the crowd, who were now looking their way.

Shanna shielded her face. Noting the warning glance from Jace, she quickened her pace.

"Well, look who's here," Boyd Davidson continued in his loud voice. "Just in time."

A murmur rippled through the crowd.

Panic gripped Shanna like a cold hand. Barstow? Here? Now? Without looking, she broke in to a run.

Jace matched her. They reached the door to the side vestibule. She grabbed the handle. Pulling it open, she glanced over her shoulder.

She expected to see the black SUV, or maybe Barstow himself, standing in the street, raising a deer rifle to his shoulder. Instead a brightly painted van pulled to the curb. A familiar-looking brunette jumped out along with a man Shanna didn't know. A man balancing a large camera on his shoulder. A news team.

And their camera was pointed right at her.

# *Chapter Eleven*

Shanna and Jace ducked into the vestibule. So much for her new identity. If that news camera was on, it had caught her on tape. Even with the new hair and sunglasses, someone could recognize her.

She might not have as much time as she hoped.

She plunged her hand into the pocket of her new coat. Locating her wallet, she dug out Linda's key card. At one side of the door was a small panel. She stood to the side, trying to avoid the camera she knew was in the console. She pushed the card into the slot and punched in Linda's number.

The machine didn't respond.

"Great. The machine picked today to malfunction." Unless she'd entered the number wrong. She removed her sunglasses and stuffed them into her coat pocket, still careful to avoid the security camera peering out of the machine. Fingers trembling, she punched in Linda's number again, focusing on each digit, making certain she had it correct.

Still, nothing.

"The machine must be broken. There's another entrance on the other side of the building. We'll have to try that one." She hit the eject button and waited for the card to spit out.

Nothing happened.

She couldn't believe this. She hit the button again. She'd beat the machine silly if it thought it was going to swallow her card.

"Shanna?" Jace stared through the glass door leading into the inside hall. At the far end of the hall, a security guard walked toward them.

Shanna's hands shook so much she could hardly control them enough to try the button again. Was this more than a malfunction? Had Barstow flagged Linda's card in some way? Had he guessed she would go to her friend for help?

She remembered the police showing up at Linda's door the night before. Maybe they'd been watching Linda's place. Maybe they were waiting for her to show.

"I hope you can get us out of this."

She hoped she could, too.

The guard drew closer. He was big, well over six feet, and his bulk blocked the dim light from inside the hall. He reached the vestibule door. Sunlight streaming in from outside illuminated a doughy face set with bright blue eyes. A thin goatee framed his thin lips.

Dirk.

"It's okay. He's a friend. I should be able to talk to him." She didn't add that Dirk had wanted more, that he asked her out at least once a month, that maybe she could use his feelings for her to her advantage. At least that was what she hoped. The fact that she was accused of killing two men and was a fugitive might lessen his attraction.

Men were funny that way.

She gave Dirk what she hoped was an embarrassed yet flirtatious smile.

He opened the door, blocking the entrance with his big frame. He stared at her for a moment, brows crunched low over his eyes. "Shanna?"

"Hi, Dirk. Don't say you didn't recognize me."

"You changed your hair."

"Do you like it?"

"It looks great. But then any way you wore your hair would look great." His thin lips curved in a smile, as if blissfully unaware he was looking at an accused murderer.

Apparently Dirk didn't watch the news.

He narrowed his eyes on Jace. "I don't think we've met."

Jace gave him a pained smile.

"This is John Sebastian, Dirk. Mr. Sebastian is working on PR for the mill project. I told him I'd let him in the side entrance so he could avoid all that." Shanna gestured toward the front of the building.

Dirk nodded to Jace. "Damn protestors."

"We need to get in to the building without attracting attention outside," Shanna said. "Can you help? I think my card is jammed."

Dirk frowned down at the machine. "It's not your card."

"Is the machine broken?"

"No. I mean, the card. It's not yours."

A small detail she'd hoped he wouldn't notice. "Yeah. I left mine in my office. Linda let me use hers so I could get in this morning. It's kind of an emergency, with the protest and everything."

"You're supposed to call security if something like that happens, Shanna. You're never supposed to use someone else's card."

"I know. I was just in a hurry. And with this mine protest business, I'm a little at loose ends."

He punched a few buttons. He frowned and hit a few more. Finally the machine coughed up the card. Dirk slipped it into his pocket. "Tell Linda to see me this morning to get her card back."

No, no, no. If Dirk made a big deal about this, it was only a matter of time before Mr. Barstow would zero in on her friend. If he hadn't already. And if that happened, she didn't know what he'd do. "Come on, Dirk. This is my fault. Not Linda's."

"Each person is responsible for their own card."

"But I talked her in to it. I pleaded with her." She could feel Jace watching her, waiting for her to talk her way out as she'd promised. She kept her eyes glued to Dirk. "You can write me up or whatever you need to do, but forget I ever had Linda's card, would you?"

Dirk scuffed his big feet on the tile floor. "I don't know, Shanna. I suppose I could fill out a report stating that you lost your card."

"And not mention Linda?"

"Her card was logged in to the machine."

"Can you log it out as if she popped in and then left?"

He hesitated. "I guess I could."

Shanna let out the breath she'd been holding. She could feel Jace's tension ease, too, though she didn't dare look at him. "Thanks, Dirk. I really appreciate this."

The big man nodded and smiled. "You'll have to come with me to the guard's station to fill out the report."

Shanna's relief vanished. The last place she wanted to go was the lobby. Not with the television cameras out front. Not with her coworkers bound to see her. Not with Mr. Barstow's inevitable entrance. "Is that necessary? We're kind of in a hurry."

Dirk looked from her to Jace. The grin dropped from his thin lips, and they twitched downward in a frown. "Who did you say this was?"

"Sebastian. Public relations," Jace said, convincingly.

At least Shanna hoped Dirk would find it convincing.

Dirk narrowed his bright blue eyes on her. "You're in accounting. What do you have to do with a PR man? And why isn't there a Sebastian on my list?"

"I'm just doing a favor for—"

"Do you think I'm stupid, Shanna?" Dirk shook his big head slowly. "I'm afraid I'm going to have to ask the two of you to come with me."

JACE SIZED UP THE GUARD. He was big, strong, probably at least somewhat trained and definitely armed. He glanced at the pistol in the behemoth's holster. It would be tough to take him. But if Shanna couldn't flirt her way out of this mess, he didn't have a lot of options.

"I can't go with you, Dirk. I'm sorry." She took a step backward, toward the door.

Dirk glanced from Shanna to Jace and back again. "What's going on, Shanna? Who is he? Really?"

"He's no one."

No one? Maybe he should be offended. Instead—in the interest of getting out of this building without having to get his butt kicked—he decided he'd try to look like no one.

Shanna shook her head, as if realizing how ridiculous she sounded. "He's just trying to help me."

The guard's frown deepened. "Why do you need help?"

"Frankly, I don't know. But I'll try to explain."

Dirk tilted his head to the side. He looked like he wanted to believe her. Like he wanted to hear her explanation. But Shanna's story was so outlandish there was no guarantee the guard could swallow it no matter how willing. Jace had certainly had some trouble. Even Linda had balked at first, and Linda was Shanna's best friend.

"You know the company hunting trip? I was invited this

year. And while we were out in the mountains, Mr. Barstow tried to shoot me."

Dirk shook his big head, as if tossing off the incongruous idea like a wet dog shakes off water.

Jace tensed. Maybe if he could get a hold of the guard's gun, he'd have a chance.

Shanna splayed her hands in front of her, palms up. "I know it sounds crazy, but hear me out. Please, Dirk?"

If Jace was the guard, he'd already be on the phone. But to his relief, the man-mountain just watched Shanna and waited for her to continue.

"I got away, but two men died. The outfitter and Mr. Davis."

"Ronald Davis?"

"Yes. Shot by Mr. Barstow. And now he's blaming their murders on me."

"Why would he do that?"

"I don't know. That's why I need to get in to my office. I think there's something I stumbled on that Mr. Barstow wants kept secret. Maybe Mr. Davis knew about it, too."

Dirk nodded, as if he was not only listening to Shanna, but also actually believing her story.

Amazing.

Obviously Dirk found Shanna attractive. How could he not? But the look in his eyes said more. The guy seemed to hold a torch for her. As long as his brain didn't kick in, maybe Shanna could talk him in to believing anything.

"The sheriff was hunting with us, too. He's in on this with Mr. Barstow."

"The sheriff? What about Palmer police?"

"They believe what they've been told. That I shot two men. That I'm a murderer. But I'm not, Dirk. You know that, don't you?"

Tension clamped down on the back of Jace's neck once again. He didn't like Shanna laying things out so clearly, asking for Dirk's trust point-blank. It was a gutsy move...and one that could easily backfire.

Dirk frowned and hunched his Wyoming-size shoulders.

Shanna touched his arm. "You know me, Dirk. You know I'm not capable of doing something like that. Never. Remember the time you killed that mouse in my office?"

Dirk's distressed expression didn't change, but he managed a laugh. "You were so upset. I would have thought it was your pet, had I not known better."

Shanna nodded. "Can you imagine me killing a person? Any person?"

Dirk met her eyes. His jaw went soft. "No."

"Then you have to let me run up to my office. Just for a few minutes. I need the chance to clear my name."

"I can't let you in. Not now that your card has been flagged."

"Can't you unflag it? Say it was a mistake?"

The big guy actually swayed on his feet, as if being pulled by two invisible and opposing forces.

"Please, Dirk. You're my only chance."

The guard pulled a notebook and pen from his jacket and scrawled a telephone number and address. He ripped out the page and handed it to Shanna. "I need to get back to the lobby, but if you need more help, you just ask."

Shanna stuffed the paper in her pocket. "Thank you, Dirk. You might have just saved my life."

The guard held the door open for Shanna to slip through. As Jace followed, the soft expression in the guard's eyes changed to challenge.

A man claiming his territory with all the subtlety of a bull elk during the rut.

Jace tried to keep his expression neutral, but something responded low in his gut. He struggled to keep his hands from balling into fists, from punching the big guard in the nose just because it would feel good.

At least he knew one thing. The guard might be promising to help Shanna, but he had plans of his own.

And those plans didn't include Jace.

SHANNA SETTLED INTO the familiar contours of her work chair and tried to focus, despite Jace's relentless pacing and peeking into the hall every other second. She was still shaking from their close call with Dirk, but what had her really jangled was how she felt she no longer belonged in her own office.

How could she have not sensed this before? How could she have spent fifty hours a week in front of this desk and not have felt the dangerous undercurrents flowing around her?

She sure felt them now.

She picked up the picture of Emily that she'd snapped on their minivacation to the Buffalo Bill Historical Center in Cody last summer. She removed the photo from its frame and slipped it into her pocket. She didn't care about the rest of her things. Let Barstow do whatever he wanted with them. But she wasn't leaving a picture of her daughter in this place. She was sorry she'd taken the job at Talbot. She was sorry she'd brought Emily into this at all.

She just prayed the files would provide a way to get her daughter out. To get them both out.

She booted up her computer and glanced up at Jace, who was still pacing her office floor. "Something's bothering you."

"I don't trust him."

"Who?"

"Your guard friend." He stopped and met her eyes, as if to check out her reaction.

She shook her head and typed in her password. She could understand why Jace was so keyed up after their close call. She'd felt his tension in the vestibule. She'd seen him eye Dirk's gun. She'd sensed him getting ready to jump the guard if Shanna hadn't been able to reach him.

Strangely enough, Shanna hadn't doubted Dirk would come around. Once she'd started explaining, she knew he'd believe her. She wanted to trust his offer of help was real. Of course, her judgment of men had proven to be lacking. "Do you think he'll call the police? Or Barstow?"

"Maybe not. But I still don't trust him. He wants something, and he thinks by helping, he can get it."

"Wants something? What?"

"You."

Her cheeks heated like a teenage girl's. She didn't know why she felt so flustered. She'd known Dirk had a crush on her for months. She'd even talked about it with Linda, no blushing involved. But this was different, and the only reason she could figure was that this time the observation was coming from Jace.

She looked down at the computer, taking a moment to regain her composure. "We needed his help to get into the building."

"And you trust him?"

"I don't know. Shouldn't I?"

"He's in this for you. How reliable do you think he'll be once he figures out you aren't interested in the same outcome as he is?"

She wanted to toss out a great comeback. Question why he thought she wasn't interested in the same thing as Dirk. But she knew Jace wouldn't buy it. And she'd never been very good at playing those games. Not when the outcome mattered.

She focused on her desktop screen. "If I can find something

in these files, I won't have to worry about what Dirk thinks. And if you're so concerned, you can help by checking through those file cabinets behind you." She pointed to the long file cabinet that ran along the back wall of the office she shared with three other accountants.

Jace walked over to the file and pulled one of the drawers open. His shoulders slumped ever so slightly. "Now, this is a load of files."

Shanna couldn't hide her smile. She was relieved the spotlight was off her and Dirk and Jace's uncomfortable questions. "A little overwhelmed?"

He grabbed a chair from one of the desks nearby and rolled it in front of the file. "You'll have to tell me where to start or I'll be here all day."

"The files are listed under each mine's approximate location."

"How about the mill?"

"Red Desert Basin Mill."

"Check."

Shanna looked back to her computer. She logged into the system and called up the files she'd worked on during the past three months.

"I don't see it here. Are you sure it's not listed under something else?"

"It's there. Keep looking." She scanned through her project list. She scanned it again, slower. "This is weird."

Jace spun in his chair, his finger marking his place in the paper files. "What is it?"

"The mill. It's not in the computer system."

"Are you sure?"

"It must be a mistake." She hit a few keys and did a system search.

It came up empty.

A crystal-sharp trill ran over her nerves. "This is impossible. It's as if the file never existed." She met Jace's eyes across the room. "Did you find it in there?"

"No. What else is missing?"

She looked down at her list. Her heart thumped hard against her ribs. Her lungs felt tight, as if she'd just finished running in high altitude. "I don't know. I don't remember. I've done a lot of projects in the past three months."

"When did you work on the mill?"

"I finished the updated profit projection maybe two weeks ago."

"What did you work on since?"

She entered the new search parameters. The mill had been a big project. With the time she'd taken off to get ready once she'd been invited on the hunt, she'd only done one project since. "I did an analysis of a mine Talbot has invested money in."

The search came up empty. "It's not here."

"What's the mine listed under in these files?"

"Hell's Half Acre Mine. It's right near the canyon."

He turned his attention to the physical files. "What did you work on before the mill?"

She conducted another search. This time, a list of files appeared. She went down the column. "There's only one more missing. Another mine not too far from the mill."

"What is that under in these files? Red Desert Basin again?"

"Yes."

"Then I can already tell you that it's not here."

She stared at the computer, her mind spinning. She tried a few more specialized searches, trying to locate any sign that the files had ever existed. Nothing.

Jace closed the file drawers. "This can't be a coincidence."

"No. Everything I've worked on in the last month is gone. Wiped from the system. It's as if the mill and the two mines never existed." She thrust herself from her chair. "So whatever it is that Barstow is trying to hide has to do with those two mines and the mill."

"Or something that happened in the past month." Jace pointed to the calendar on her desk. "Grab the pages from the last month or so. Maybe it will jog your memory."

She paged through previous weeks and ripped them off the calendar. "At least they didn't think to take these. Of course, that might mean they aren't worth taking."

"Take them anyway. With the files gone we need all the help we can get."

She stuffed the calendar pages into her coat pocket. "None of this makes sense. What possible reason would they have for deleting the files? The company is trying to get the mill up and running. That's no secret. Why would they want to pretend it doesn't exist?"

"Maybe they just want to pretend the records you saw don't exist. Was there something sensitive in those records? Something that might keep the mill from opening?"

"You mean, something the protestors could use?"

"Exactly."

She searched her memory but came up empty. "The environmental groups are worried about safety, radiation, ground water, that sort of thing. Like I said before, I don't have anything to do with that part of Talbot. I never see those reports."

"Then maybe there are financial concerns about the mill. Things that the protestors could use to stall the reopening, even if it has little to do with the mill's safety."

She shook her head. "The mill's financing is solid. It's running in the red now, but when it's operational it will bring a lot of money into Talbot."

"I remember Talbot releasing that news a while ago. It was the reason its stock price went up so dramatically. Hell, even I invested in the company."

Shanna nodded. She had, too, as part of her retirement package. As did most of Talbot's other employees. "As long as the mill opens, it will be a huge boon for the company."

"What about the mines? What do you remember about them?"

"The mines are a different story."

"How so?"

"Debt. Both mines are drowning in it. Luckily neither is actually owned by Talbot. I recommended Talbot pull out its investment of the Hell's Half Acre mine."

"So maybe that's it."

"That I recommended they pull the company out?" She shook her head. "I don't see how that could have a bearing on anything."

"What if the company that owns the mine goes out of business?"

She shook her head. All this risking their necks and brainstorming and they'd come up with nothing. "If Heritage Mining goes under, there will be jobs lost. But that doesn't really hurt Talbot in any way. I don't see why Mr. Barstow would care."

"The little guy suffers, but as long as Barstow can still afford his vacation homes…" The bitterness in Jace's voice was unmistakable.

At least now she knew where it came from. "Who knows, if they can get the mill up and running, they might even be able to turn the mines around. There isn't much refining capacity in—"

Jace held up a hand. He touched his index finger to his lips and shot her a warning look.

She sucked in a breath and held it.

The low rumble of a man's voice emanated from the hall outside. "I'm checking again right now. If it's not here, it has to be somewhere in her apartment. I'll call you back."

Shanna sucked in a breath. She knew that voice, that whisper. The last time she'd heard it, she was hiding under a shelf of rock on Gusset Ridge.

She watched as it began and ended.

"Okay," John said. "I can see what you mean. Fill in the
caption in the lower right." He drew it in, and when it was
to be "continues to the system," and I will call you back."

Shanna did as he said. She knew that it was that she
got the feeling she'd found. She was in this work to get
to you, the Barstow Hotel.

# *Chapter Twelve*

Shanna's mouth went dry. Her heart launched into double-
time. Mr. Barstow was outside her office. He was here.

They needed to run.

She looked down at her computer. It would take too long
to shut it down. She closed the file she'd been examining and
hit the off button. She bolted out of her chair. Motioning for
Jace to follow, she made for the door that led to the office of
Mr. Davis's assistant.

Jace followed.

Before closing the door, Shanna took one last glance back.
The file cabinet was closed, the computer off. Unless Mr. Barstow turned on her computer, he'd never know she hadn't shut
it down properly. Even then, he couldn't be sure it was her
that did it. At least not right away. That should give them at
least enough time to clear the building....

Her gaze landed on the picture frame.

It lay on her desk, right where she'd left it when she'd removed Em's photo.

A wave of nausea washed through her. Mr. Barstow would
see it. He'd have to. And then he'd know.

She took a reflexive step back into the office.

Jace grabbed her hand.

The hall door's knob turned.

Shanna reversed direction, pulling herself back with Jace's help, and ducked back into the executive assistant's office.

She looked up at Jace, wanting to warn him. "The picture. He'll know." She mouthed the words more than voiced them, but he seemed to understand. He launched into motion, racing across the room. He paused at the far side, unsure which door to choose.

Shanna forced the image of Mr. Barstow in her office from her mind and took the lead, racing out the door that connected this part of the suite to the main hall. The damage was done. They had to get out of here.

They reached the main hall. Jace flattened his back to the doorjamb and peered around the corner. He nodded to signal the hall was clear, then another nod to let her know he would follow.

Blood hummed in Shanna's ears. She forced herself to think. To focus.

If Mr. Barstow was on to them, he'd expect them in the elevator or the closest staircase. They couldn't do what he expected. It was a longer run to the far stairs, but once they reached the bottom, they'd almost be outside. They'd also come out smack in the middle of the protestors.

Perfect.

She slipped into the hall and ran. She felt Jace's glance as she dashed past the first staircase. To his credit, he didn't falter, didn't slow.

She reached the far stairs and yanked open the stairwell door. Just as they slipped inside, she heard a noise behind them. Footsteps. A shout.

She gripped the cold railing. Moving her feet as fast as she could, she concentrated on hitting each step. The last thing she needed to do was fall. It would be all over then.

By the time they reached the bottom, her lungs burned for oxygen. She burst from the staircase. Jace was right behind her. She raced for the morning sun streaming in through the glass.

Voices erupted from behind. Dirk, another security guard, Mr. Barstow—she couldn't tell. She didn't care. No matter who it was, she wasn't about to stop.

She pushed through two sets of glass doors and raced into the daylight. Protestors gathered around the entrance, placards raised for the cameras. There was no way Mr. Barstow could follow them through this crowd. As soon as the protestors spotted him, they'd pounce.

She headed right for the middle. She could feel Jace on her heels. She didn't know where the news camera was or if it caught their escape. She supposed it didn't matter. Mr. Barstow knew she was in Palmer. He knew she was working to find the truth. And now that he knew, the sheriff would know, as well.

She had already run out of time.

They reached the bikes, climbed on and started the engines. They raced down streets and around corners, putting distance between them and Talbot, them and Mr. Barstow. The shrill little motor buzzed in Shanna's ears, finally drowning out the thrum of her pulse.

Jace pulled alongside and motioned for her to follow. She let him take the lead. They crossed the river. At the far side of the bridge, he slowed to a crawl and jumped off. He wheeled the motorbike off the side of the road and stopped in the shelter of the bridge.

Shanna stopped beside him. Her legs felt weak. Her throat was impossibly dry. She stood and panted, unable to do anything else.

Jace's dark eyes drilled into her. "What's in your apartment? What is Barstow looking for?"

She leaned against her bike. If she didn't have it to hold on to, she would have fallen over, she would have collapsed to the rocky ground in a heap. "I don't know."

"Think. Did you bring something home from the office? Files? Paperwork?"

She shook her head. She couldn't focus. All she could think of was Barstow. All she could hear was the quiet ring of his voice. She forced herself to breathe slowly, deeply. "I work on my laptop. I have some files on my laptop."

"Is it in your apartment?"

She nodded. She could see right where it was. "My bedroom closet."

Jace frowned, as if what she'd said didn't add up. "The police should have gone through your apartment right away. I would think they'd have taken it."

Shanna tried to remember what she'd done before she'd left on the hunting trip. "It's in the back of my bedroom closet. Maybe they just haven't seen it."

"More likely they haven't executed a search warrant yet." Jace nodded as if he'd figured out the answer. "There's something on it, all right. At least Barstow thinks there is. And he wants to get it before the Palmer police and sheriff's deputies get in the mix. He probably asked the sheriff to delay the official search until he finds that laptop. And you know what that means?"

Shanna's mind was still back in her office, back waiting for Mr. Barstow to step through that door. She shook her head.

"It means I'm going to get it before they do."

His words ripped through Shanna with the force of a bullet. "You can't! They'll catch you!"

He held out his hand. "Key?"

Shanna slipped her hand into her pocket and touched her apartment key. She didn't pull it out. "It's too dangerous."

"If it is, I'll drive away. They don't know me. Not if your guard friend didn't give them my description. In fact, in case he did…" He pulled his hat off his head and placed it on Shanna's. "Keep it safe for me, would you?"

"You can't take a chance like that. Not for my sake."

"I'm already taking a chance."

"Not like this." She had to make him see what he was doing. "Just last night you were afraid I was going to sell you out. Now you're walking into my apartment in front of the police?"

"You said it yourself, Shanna. If we can find the answers— the answers Barstow seems to believe are on your laptop— all of this goes away. The threat to you. The threat to me. The threat to your daughter. Think about it. Now that Barstow knows you're here in Palmer, what do you think he's going to do?"

Her heart stuttered.

"That's right. He'll go after Emily. He'll use her to get to you."

She held up a shaking hand. "Stop."

"I think protecting Emily is worth taking a chance, don't you?" He held out his hand once more. "The key."

What could she do? She closed her fist around her apartment key and pulled it from her pocket. She dropped it into his open hand and gave him the address. "Be careful. Please."

He stuffed the key into his own pocket and leaned toward her. Slipping his hand around the back of her head, he brought his lips to hers.

His kiss was quick, yet the heat behind it burned to her toes. When he released her, she stepped backward, her lips hot, her skin tingling from his light beard. She propped herself up with the dirt bike, unable to regain her balance, unable to catch her breath.

"I'll see you at the cabin." Jace climbed up the bank to the road and threw a leg over his bike. A flick of the switch and the motor revved to life. He buzzed onto the road and out of sight.

Shanna brought her fingertips to her lips. She had to trust Jace would be okay, that he wouldn't take the chance if it became too dangerous, that he'd return to the cabin. She couldn't worry about him. Not now. Because he was right. Emily was in danger.

And Shanna would do whatever it took to protect her little girl.

JACE SPOTTED the unmarked police car from a block away.

When he was a detective, he'd often driven his own car for that very reason. Any thug worth spit could spot an unmarked. He guessed now that he was working on the other side of what passed for the law, he must have developed the same skill.

What a proud moment.

He slipped into an alley three buildings down and left the dirt bike leaning against the bear fence surrounding the garbage cans. From there, it was only a matter of traipsing through backyards to reach the rear entrance of Shanna's building, use the key she'd given him to let himself in, find apartment 2B, get the laptop and get out—all without attracting the notice of the boys out front.

Piece of cake.

Jace made it into the building without being spotted. He climbed the stairs to the second floor and found Shanna's apartment. He turned the key in the door marked 2B and let himself in.

So far, so good.

The air felt heavy, as if no life had stirred it for a while. But that was the only thing about the place that seemed lifeless. Although the walls were still standard apartment white, artwork was everywhere, from colorful depictions of unchecked childhood imagination covering the refrigerator to prints inspired by the beautiful Wyoming landscape hung on the living-room walls, every surface felt hopeful and upbeat.

Like Shanna herself.

He pressed his lips together. He shouldn't have kissed her, but he hadn't been able to stop himself. She'd honestly seemed worried about him. Not because of what he could do for her, but because she cared. Really cared.

He shook his head. He shouldn't be so trusting, so eager to believe she felt something for him. Not that he thought Shanna was deceptive—she was one of the most honest women he'd ever met—but he'd witnessed her play up to good old Dirk to get what she desperately needed. She was capable of manipulation. That was clear. The thing that confused him was why he felt so sure her feelings for him were real.

Wishful thinking?

He forced his feet to move past the living room and kitchen and down the hall toward the bedrooms. When it came down to it, Shanna's feelings didn't really matter. Darla had loved him, of that he had no doubt. Yet when she had no other options, she'd still thrown him under the bus. He knew the decision she'd been forced to make would haunt her the rest of her life, but that didn't change anything. Her kids came first, as well they should. And he could say the same thing about Shanna.

When push came to shove, she'd choose Emily over her own life. Certainly she wouldn't let Jace get in the way, whether she cared for him or not.

Reaching the first bedroom door, he slowed his steps and

peered inside. A riotous explosion of pink and green flowers danced on the walls. A frilly white bedspread and stuffed animals covered the narrow bed. And on one wall, a poster of the Power Rangers stared back at him. He reached a hand into his coat pocket. His fingers brushed the little plastic man.

He couldn't help but smile.

He might be crazy for coming to Shanna's apartment, for stretching his neck out for the blade. But maybe a little risk was the price you paid for having a little girl look at you as if you were some kind of hero. Maybe you start doing crazy things just to avoid letting her—and her mother—down.

He continued down the hall to the last room. The first thing he focused on was the bed. Queen-sized. Lush. Soft with a down comforter and, he'd wager, a feather bed underneath.

The perfect kind of bed for making love.

He shook the thought from his mind. Not only was it stupid to torture himself with fantasies that would never come true, it was a waste of time. And right now, he didn't have an extra second.

Pulling his eyes from the bed, he stepped into the room and made for the closet.

Down the hall behind him, a key rattled in the apartment door.

# Chapter Thirteen

One ring…two…

Shanna clasped one of the few pay phones in town to her ear and prayed her friend hadn't already left to take Emily to the babysitter. She would have driven to Linda's house, but no matter how fast she pushed the little dirt bike, she'd been afraid she wouldn't make it in time. Not that calling wasn't a huge risk. From where she was standing, she could see the convenience store's security camera recording her image.

She tried to angle her head downward, using the brim of Jace's hat to hide her features. Not that it mattered. She'd rather risk being seen than let Linda show up at work. There was no telling how much danger she'd gotten her friend in.

Three rings…four…

"Hello?"

"Linda. You've got to listen."

"Shanna? Where are you? What's going on?" Linda sounded more shaken than she had the night before. After the police had shown up at her door and she'd heard details of the allegations against Shanna on the news, her friend was probably frightened out of her mind.

Guilt nibbled at the back of Shanna's still-aching neck. Unfortunately she was about to make it worse. "You can't go in to work today."

"What?"

"You can't go to Talbot."

"What happened?" Linda's voice was a mix of alarm and concern.

"They know I was there. They know I used your card."

"Shanna! You said no one will know, you said—"

"I know what I said, and I'm sorry. Things didn't go as smoothly as I planned." Understatement of the year. She'd screwed up big-time. She just hoped to God she didn't drag her friend down with her. "Mr. Barstow showed up while Jace and I were going through the records in my office."

"Barstow? This early? Did he know you were there? Does he know you used my card?"

"I don't know what Mr. Barstow knows about your card. But he knows I was there. He might find out how I got in. Or at least how I tried to get in."

"Okay, now you've totally lost me."

Across the store, the clerk checked her out. Shanna pressed the phone closer to her mouth. She knew the guy probably wasn't reading her lips. He likely didn't even recognize her, not with her new hair and the cowboy hat covering most of her face. But she worried all the same. "Remember Dirk Simon? The security guard? I couldn't get your card to work. I think I must have sent off some kind of alarm in the computer system. Dirk was the guard who responded. He agreed to help me."

"You explained the situation to him? The whole thing?"

"Yes. And he believed me."

"Are you sure? Sounds like Dirk could be the reason Mr. Barstow showed up so conveniently."

She imagined Jace would agree with Linda's assessment.

"I don't know. I don't think so. I don't know why, but I feel like Dirk was serious about helping me."

Linda made a humming noise in the phone, as if she wasn't so sure.

"You know he likes me."

"Wanting to get into your pants and agreeing to help a person wanted for a double murder are two different things, Shanna."

"Maybe you're right."

"First you're relying on that cowboy, now a security guard. There are no heroes in this world. Not anymore. You should know that better than anyone."

Linda was right. She should know better. About Dirk and about Jace. Maybe she was still being naive. She could just imagine what Linda would say if she knew about Jace's kiss. And the way Shanna hungered for more.

Too bad she'd be keeping those details to herself.

In the background, Shanna could hear Emily's voice. "Is that Mommy?" She sounded so little. Like a baby. A sweet, vulnerable baby.

Tears clogged Shanna's throat and distorted her vision. She opened her eyes wide so they wouldn't spill down her cheeks.

"Are you still there?" Linda demanded.

Shanna cleared her throat. "This will be over soon, Linda. I promise."

"Will I still have my job?" Linda's voice rang hard over the phone.

Her friend had every right to be angry. Shanna had screwed up. She'd talked Linda in to taking a big risk, then she'd blown it. "I'm so sorry, Linda. I didn't mean to bring you into this."

"No, I'm sorry." Linda's voice was softer. "I know you didn't do it on purpose. I know none of this is your fault."

Maybe the trouble she was in wasn't her fault, but getting Linda involved was. Now Shanna had endangered her friend, and by extension she'd brought even more peril to her little girl. "Can you go somewhere, Linda? Somewhere no one will find you?"

"Just leave?"

"Yes. With Emily. Is there somewhere you could take her where both of you will be safe?"

Linda was silent for a moment.

Shanna eyed the clerk, who was now openly staring at her. She tilted the hat brim a little lower. She had to get her point across to Linda and then get out of there before the guy called the police. "You have to leave, Linda. You have to hide. You and Emily."

"I suppose I could go to my mother's."

Shanna's stomach tightened. Linda hated her mother. Hated the tiny trailer she lived in. Hated the poverty and hopelessness of the bleak little corner of the small town where she'd grown up. Yet she was willing to go there to keep Emily safe. Because of the danger Shanna had put them both in. And only Shanna knew how much that decision had cost her friend. "Thank you, Lin. I owe you."

ADRENALINE SPIKED Jace's blood and made his mind race. He looked through the door of Shanna's bedroom and down the hall. Had Barstow made it to Shanna's apartment already? Or had Jace been spotted by the officer outside?

He heard the lock click open and the door swing wide. Hell.

He dashed for the closet. As quietly as he could, he slid the mirrored closet door open. Controlling his breathing, he strained to hear.

Heavy footsteps crossed the tile of the entry area.

He pushed his way into the closet, between a silky blouse and the nubbiness of tweed. Shanna's light floral fragrance filled his senses, her scent permeating the clothing. He slid the door shut. It stuck with an inch to go.

The footsteps grew muffled, padding across carpet, heading this way.

Whoever was out there, he was close. In the hall? In the room? Jace couldn't tell.

"I'll start in the bedroom."

Not Barstow. The sheriff. A man who was armed, trained, a man who would be tougher to overpower.

Still, the physical work on his ranch had made Jace hard and fit. Maybe he could take the guy. Keep him from reaching his gun. With the element of surprise on his side, it might be possible.

All he could hear was the beat of his own pulse, the rasp of his own breath. From the crack in the door, Jace could see a bedside table covered in lace that boasted a photo of Emily. He couldn't see Gable, but he knew the sheriff had entered the room. He also knew it wouldn't take the man long to decide to check the closet.

Jace shifted his feet, trying to work his way deeper into the clothing. His boot hit something solid. Carefully bending down, his fingers brushed the zipper of some kind of case.

The laptop. It was sitting at his feet.

If he could overpower the sheriff...if he could grab the laptop and run...

There had to be something he could use as a weapon. He groped around the closet, his hand brushing soft clothing. He touched the hard edge of a small box.

Shoes.

He slipped his hand under the lid. He could only hope Shanna liked stilettos. His fingers touched some kind of alligator-embossed leather…and a heel. A long, spiky, strong heel. He took a shoe out of the box and tested the weight of it in his hand.

"Find anything?" a voice boomed from the doorway.

Barstow. It had to be.

Jace let out the breath he'd been holding. As nice a weapon as the shoe made, it would be no match for two men. Especially two as fit as the sheriff and Barstow.

He was in deep trouble.

"Nope. Nothing yet."

"You try the closet?"

Jace's heart slammed hard enough to break a rib. He grabbed the laptop's case and moved it to the outer edge of the closet, pushing it up to the door.

A dark shape blocked his view of the room. Broad shoulders. An expensive topcoat.

Flattening his body against the back wall, Jace sucked in a lungful of Shanna's sweet scent and held it.

The door slid open. "Here it is." A hand bearing a huge platinum ring grabbed the case's handle and picked it up.

Jace didn't dare move, he didn't dare breathe. A drop of sweat trickled down his back. Another followed.

Finally the wall shuddered with the force of the front door slamming closed.

"WHERE IN THE HELL were you?" Jace knew he sounded like a jealous husband, but he couldn't help it. When he'd returned to the cabin and Shanna hadn't been there, he'd feared the worst. He'd been so relieved when he'd heard the buzz of the motorbike outside, he'd met Shanna in the garage.

Shanna parked her bike in the space next to Jace's. She took his hat off her head and handed it to him. "I had to call Linda. I had to warn her not to go in to work today."

Of course. He plopped the hat on his head. If he hadn't been so focused on getting the laptop before Barstow, he might have thought of that, too. He was glad Shanna had been a little more clearheaded. "And she took the advice?"

"She's going to bring Emily to her mother's place and stay until this blows over."

"No one will look for her there?"

"She hasn't had much to do with her mother over the years. I don't think she's told anyone but me where she grew up."

"Why the secret?"

"She didn't have an easy life. And she was worried about assumptions people might make if they knew where she came from."

"Wrong side of the tracks?"

"Something like that."

Apparently Linda had done all right for herself. "Why did it take so long?"

"The clerk in the convenience store might have recognized me. I drove off in the opposite direction and doubled back so he couldn't tell the police where I was headed."

"Smart." Shanna really was amazing. Every time he started to think he had to take care of her, she did something so sharp or brave, it put his worries to shame. "Sounds like we both had close calls."

"Did you get the laptop?"

The gut ache that had assaulted him after his near run-in with Barstow and the sheriff returned full force. "They beat me to it."

The hopeful gleam in Shanna's eyes dimmed. "So Mr. Barstow has that, too."

She looked as frustrated as he'd felt on the way back from her apartment. He'd had time to think since then, brainstorm a way around Barstow's seeming invulnerability. "There still might be a way. We could go to the source."

"You mean, the mines and mill themselves?"

"Exactly."

She pressed her lips into a grim line and shook her head. "I don't visit the sites as part of my job, you know. If anything is out of place, I doubt I'll be able to recognize it."

He'd thought of that. And maybe his idea was little more than a Hail Mary. But from where they were standing, there wasn't much else they could do. "Maybe it will be nothing. But it's worth a shot. Besides, now that the authorities know you're in Palmer, it might be a good time to leave. Even just for a few hours."

"Like a minivacation from being hunted." She gave him a tense smile.

Jace returned it. "Yeah, something like that." What he wouldn't give to just cut loose and kiss her again. When he'd done it the first time, he'd thought it was possible he'd never see her again. When he'd returned to the cabin to find she still wasn't back, he believed he'd been right.

The weight of relief suddenly bore down on his shoulders. He turned away from Shanna and walked back into the cabin. He had to get his head straight. He'd been alone for so long, not willing to let any part of his life be dependent on someone else. Not willing to give anyone power to affect him. Maybe this desire for Shanna was pure loneliness. Plain old-fashioned sex drive.

But he was afraid it was more.

He took off his hat and tossed it down on the counter top. Turning on the tap, he splashed his face. The water's cold slap felt invigorating, refreshing, but it failed to wash away his errant thoughts or divert his focus.

He could hear Shanna moving around in the kitchen behind him. He could feel each look she directed his way. He burned to ask if she felt the same thing he did...the attraction, the tenderness, the almost overpowering need. Yet he knew no matter how she answered, it wouldn't change a thing.

He would still be taking a huge risk. He would still be surrendering control. He would still be putting himself smack in the middle of the same situation that had nearly killed him before.

And yet when he looked into her eyes, when he smelled her scent, when he heard the tones of her voice, everything he knew ceased to matter.

He turned off the water and ripped a paper towel from the roll near the sink. He took his time blotting his face. He needed to focus. On their next move. On making Barstow and Gable pay. On ending this whole mess before he dug himself too deep to climb out. "There's one problem."

"Only one?"

Only one he could afford to acknowledge at the moment. "We need a vehicle." The dirt bikes worked well for running the few miles into town. But Red Desert Basin and Hell's Half Acre weren't just a few miles away. They were talking serious road trip.

"I can pay you back when this is over. Do you have the money?"

"Not without going to a bank." Which meant records. Which meant their chances of being tracked—of his identity being discovered by police—increased dramatically. "I might have to steal one."

She nodded, no flinch, no sign of guilt. Only yesterday the

thought of stealing wheels was unacceptable to her. Another sign of how desperation could change a person.

"Or…"

"Or what?"

"Dirk did say he'd help." A crease formed between her eyebrows, as if she wasn't too sure about her pal, Dirk.

Jace weighed the idea. He might live to regret this. But if they played it right, even if things went wrong, they shouldn't be in a worse position than they were in now. "You still have his number?"

She dipped her hand into her pocket and pulled out the piece of paper. "What if Dirk is the one who called Mr. Barstow? What if that's why he showed up so early?"

"I thought you believed he wanted to help."

"I've been known to be wrong about people's intentions." She tilted a shoulder. "Quite a lot lately."

Or maybe circumstances had merely pounded the trust out of her. He'd sure been there. He just hated seeing it happen to Shanna. "Ask him to drop off his car at that little park along the river. We'll be there ahead of time, make sure he isn't followed. I know just the place. If someone comes looking for us or sets up a roadblock, we'll know."

"We need to find a phone."

"We'll buy one. A disposable cell. I have enough money left for that. And it might just come in handy."

"Okay." She nodded and started for the garage. "Let's go."

He watched her cross the kitchen, taking in the determined set of her jaw, the sway of her hips. This wild ride could end at any time. With an arrest. With a bullet. If they could pull off some kind of miracle, maybe even with justice. But all he could think about at this moment was how much he'd regret not getting another taste of Shanna before it did.

God help him.

## Chapter Fourteen

Shanna wasn't surprised at all when Dirk agreed to lend them his car. But she still couldn't get over the fact that Jace had gone along with the idea. On his lunch break, Dirk had left his car at the park, then started the walk back to the Talbot building. Jace and Shanna watched him from an elevated spot on the opposite riverbank until he was nothing but a speck on the road.

No sign of anyone following. No sign of roadblocks. After Jace looked the car over, they were on their way.

Shanna expected sirens to sound any moment on the drive to the Red Desert Basin, but they never did. After that, she started to feel strangely relaxed. As she sat in the passenger seat watching the desertlike plains whiz by, she could almost pretend they were just going out to take in the sights of Wyoming.

Or maybe she was too exhausted from days of being on the run that she no longer had the energy to be afraid.

However, after uneventful stops at the business-as-usual mine and the still-closed mill in the Red Desert Basin, Shanna's mood turned to despair. As they circled north to Casper then headed west through the blink of a town called Powder River, the prospect that they might find nothing of value weighed heavy on her shoulders. "Maybe this is a waste of time."

The sun was already getting low in the west. Jace squinted and pulled his hat lower as they drove into it. "We won't know until you can take a look at that last mine."

"And see what?" She let out a frustrated breath. Jace didn't seem to understand what her job actually entailed. "I don't know what I'm seeing. My job is crunching numbers, not checking out the actual mill and mines. All I could tell you about the operations in the Red Desert Basin is what you saw yourself."

"Maybe this next one will be different."

She shook her head. "I don't understand what you're hoping I'll see."

He glanced at her again. The sun shined harsh on his face. Dark circles cupped under his eyes. The stubble on his chin had grown into a full-fledged beard. He looked tired, as tired as she felt. "I don't know, Shanna. I wish we'd been able to find something in the Talbot computer. I wish I'd been able to get a hold of your laptop. I'm out of ideas, but I'll be damned if I'm going to let another rich bastard get away with murder. And I'll be damned if I'm going to stand around and do nothing while you are hunted down like an animal."

Shanna flattened herself to the back of her seat. The passion in his voice shook her to the core. From the beginning she'd known Jace had his reasons for helping her, reasons that had more to do with the kind of man Mr. Barstow was than any kind of feelings for her.

But now she wasn't so certain.

He still had his own reasons, to be sure. But she had a strong feeling that he'd added her to the list…her and Em, of course. Maybe even put them up near the top. She could hear it in his voice.

And something deep inside her responded. "You're right. Maybe I'll see something. I'll give it my best."

"That's my girl."

A shiver settled in her chest. His girl. She wasn't sure how that should make her feel. Indignant, maybe. The thought that she belonged to him, that she was a girl and not a woman. But somehow she couldn't muster any of those feelings. Instead, she wanted to wrap her arms around those words and hold them to her heart.

For however long she could.

Up ahead, the flat plains of sage yawned. The ground split and opened into a chasm. Hell's Half Acre was really a horseshoe gorge encompassing 320 acres of badlands in the middle of nowhere. A wound in the earth formed by an ancient offshoot of the Powder River, a bit like a miniature Grand Canyon.

She pointed to a dirt road leading off the highway before they reached the badlands. The shortest route to the mine. "There."

Jace took the turn. The car bounced over ruts in the road.

Shanna held on to the dash, each jolt hitting her like a kick to the kidneys. "God, I hate off-road driving."

"This road is in good shape, for a mining road."

She looked at him. "Are you serious?"

Jace shrugged a shoulder. "You saw all the trucks on the road leading to the Red Desert Basin mine. This doesn't look nearly as well-traveled."

He was probably right. Now that she really looked, she could see that in some places, sage encroached on the dirt tracks…nature's attempt to reclaim her land. "This road curves back around to the highway. Maybe the trucks use the other side more." Though why they wouldn't use the shorter route, she couldn't say.

"Maybe." Jace kept driving. The road started to curve, as she'd said. At one point it drew close to the canyon, exposing its colorful layers of striated rock. A sheer cliff overlooking what seemed like an alien landscape. Jace gestured to the badlands. "It's something, isn't it? Totally different feel from the mountains, but beautiful all the same."

Shanna wished she could share in Jace's appreciation. But she was too busy scanning the sage-covered plains. They crested another hill, and the prairie stretched out before them.

She sucked in a sharp breath. "Stop."

Jace brought the car to a halt. "What is it?"

Her eyes combed the gentle roll of land. She'd worked on this account for weeks. She'd studied the maps. This was the place. She knew it. "It's not here."

"What's not here?"

"The mine." She threw open her door and climbed out. She wove around clumps of sage. "The mine should be right here."

The car engine turned off and a door slammed behind her. Jace caught her at the top of a gentle swell. "It's probably up ahead. We haven't reached it yet."

"Do you see anything up ahead?"

He didn't answer. There was no answer to give.

"It's supposed to be right here." She gestured to the untouched ground in front of her. "When the mine was proposed, several groups protested the fact that it was so close to Hell's Half Acre."

"Maybe there's another point in the road that runs this close."

"No. There isn't." She pointed to the dirt road. "See how it curves away? It keeps going in that direction."

Jace squinted, scanning the landscape. "And you're sure this is the right road?"

"I'm sure." She hadn't physically visited this mine before,

but she had a head for geography. "I've seen the map a thousand times."

"Maybe the controversy wasn't resolved and the mine never got up and running."

"No. It was resolved. Or at least the protestors' claims were disregarded. That's why the company that actually operates the mine went to Talbot. Heritage Mining. They needed Talbot's help to push the permits through. Mr. Barstow is good at that."

"I'll bet."

"Besides, this mine is racking up debt like you wouldn't believe. The kind of debt a mine might have if it's operating full bore but not finding a single atom of uranium. That's why I recommended Talbot cut ties with Heritage Mining."

"So if the mine doesn't exist, Heritage Mining is ripping Talbot off."

"Right."

"I'll bet I can guess who owns that company."

A shiver worked its way over her skin. He didn't have to say the name. "It seems likely Mr. Barstow is behind it, doesn't it? Maybe I was never supposed to see the details of this account. Maybe Ron Davis screwed up when he assigned it to me."

"I guess he paid for his mistake."

She nodded, but she hadn't really heard. "A dummy company. A convenient way to embezzle."

Jace touched her arm. "You're thinking of your ex-husband?"

She tried to wave away his concern. "When I met with the SEC agent about Kurt last week, I thought I was finally done dealing with this kind of crap. Now Mr. Barstow…I just can't seem to dig myself out."

"Just because your ex-husband was an idiot, and your boss is a murderer, that doesn't say anything about you."

"Doesn't it? They used me. They took advantage of me."

"Because you're a good person."

"You mean, a gullible person."

"No. That's not what I mean. You're not gullible. You just give people the benefit of the doubt. If they don't deserve it, it's not your problem. You can't take responsibility for their choices."

She turned away, not wanting Jace to see the tears welling in her eyes. A sob pushed at the back of her throat. Not a sob of sadness or distress. More one of anger. Of frustration. Of exhaustion.

She was so tired. Tired of being a victim. Tired of being a scapegoat. Tired of being afraid.

Jace stepped up close behind her. He wrapped his arms around her middle, holding her against his hard chest.

The warmth soaked into her like rain into the desert floor. She didn't want to move. She didn't want to think. She turned around, still in his embrace, and looked up into his eyes. "I don't want to go back. Not yet."

He watched her, saying nothing, as if waiting to see what would happen next.

"Did you ever want to…escape?"

"Yes."

Of course he did. He'd told her about it. The wealthy man in Denver. His partner selling him out. God, he'd even spent time in jail. All reasons he'd moved to Wyoming.

Too bad she couldn't move. Too bad she couldn't just disappear, start a new life somewhere with Emily…somewhere with Jace.

Not possible with a double murder charge following her.

So maybe she couldn't leave her problems behind. Not

forever. But if she could for a few moments…just for a little while…

She reached her hands toward him and rested her fingers on his belt buckle. She knew the move was forward. She'd never been so forward in her life. But she was tired of responding to what others had planned. She wanted to feel strong. She wanted to be in control. "I want you, Jace. I want to feel something besides fear."

## Chapter Fifteen

Jace looked into Shanna's eyes and let the sweetness of her scent shift through his mind. He didn't know what would happen once they returned to Palmer. What the information they'd found would change. What, if anything, would happen to Barstow. But at this moment, none of that mattered. All that mattered was this moment. This feeling.

The promise of seeing Shanna's eyes without fear.

He ran his hands down her arms and lowered his mouth to hers. This time his kiss wasn't quick, but warm and slow. He nibbled her lips, teased open her mouth, tangled his tongue with hers. She tasted sweet and hot and needy. His body responded, stirring to life, pressing for release.

He could feel her hands still at his belt. She unfastened the buckle. She touched him through his jeans. He stirred, blood rushing to his groin, heat thrumming through his veins.

She peeled his jeans down his legs. Right there on the open prairie. "I've always been timid before. I don't want to be that way anymore." She fitted her hand over the bulge in his boxer briefs.

Jace buried his fingers in her hair. He murmured deep in his throat, unable to find words to answer.

Shanna slipped her fingertips under the waistband of the

underwear and pulled them down, over his hips, over his erection, down to his thighs.

He was ready for her, more than ready. He jutted toward her as if asking to be taken.

She darted her tongue between her lips and flicked him.

He responded, flexing upward. He moved his hips forward without thinking, as if his body was no longer under his control.

She licked him again, slower. Taking her time, she ran her tongue all the way up the underside of his shaft. Reaching the tip, she looked up into his eyes.

He clenched his teeth. He was going to lose it, just like that, faster than a teenaged boy.

He plunged his fingers into her hair, stopping her before she tore him apart. "Slower. Unless you want this to be over very quickly."

She gave him a mischievous grin, as if she didn't intend to listen to a thing he had to say.

A surge of want shot through him, followed by searing heat. He wanted her naked. At least he wanted to control that. He wanted to see her. All of her.

He grasped her shirt. She pulled her arms from the sleeves, and Jace helped her slip it over her head. She stripped off her bra, exposing herself.

The sun caressed untanned skin. Her breasts were beautiful. Round, soft, with nipples that peaked as if taunting him to take them in his mouth.

But Shanna had other ideas.

She ran her tongue over him again. Then moving closer, she took him between her breasts.

He drove his hips upward. She slid down his shaft until he thrust free. She took him in her mouth, sucking him, fondling him with the moist heat of her tongue.

A groan shuddered from his chest.

She slid up his length, enveloping him once again. Her nipples grazed his belly.

He'd totally lost control now. Not just of his body, but of his heart, his mind, his soul. He couldn't get enough of her. He'd never be able to get enough.

And if he'd ever hoped to get out of this unscathed, that hope was now utterly gone.

Once he'd regained his strength, he caught her, a hand on either side of her waist, and lifted her to her feet. He'd made her a promise, and he meant to keep it. "My turn."

He guided her to the car and set her on the hood. He peeled her jeans down her legs, then her panties, leaving her totally bare.

For a moment, he just looked at her. He could hardly believe how gorgeous she was, how much he wanted her, needed her. More than he ever thought he could need a woman. He ran his hands over her breasts and down her sides. He pulled her hips to the edge of the hood and lowered his mouth, ready to give her everything she'd given him.

Wanting to give her more.

He couldn't get enough of her taste, her heat, the way she responded to him. He let his tongue dance over her, devour her. She shuddered under his touch.

Her fingers gripped his shoulders, pulling him away from her, pulling him up. "I want you, Jace. I want more. I want you inside."

He rubbed his hands over her thighs and slipped his hips between them. He was ready. More than ready. Positioning himself at her entrance, he eased into her slick heat. Her body hugged him...incredibly, impossibly soft. More than he could dream.

He thrust into her, withdrew and thrust again. His vision

narrowed until he could see only Shanna, feel only Shanna. As if she was the only thing in the world that mattered. He muttered her name.

She smiled and arched her back, thrusting her breasts to the open sky. No fear. No worry. Just pure pleasure.

It was the most beautiful sight he'd ever seen.

"Hey, Dirk," Shanna said into the cell phone. "Your car is at—"

Jace pulled the key from the ignition but didn't move to get out. He could hear the sharp tone of Dirk's voice over the phone, but he couldn't decipher the words.

"What happened?" Shanna glanced at Jace. The crease appeared between her brows once again. Her lips pressed together until they were as pale as her cheeks. Now that they were back in Palmer, the fear Jace had done his best to chase away was obviously back in force.

Jace touched her hand, gently urging the phone away from her ear at an angle. He pressed his head against hers to listen in.

Dirk's voice sounded too loud, either excited or afraid. "This could be big, bigger than you thought."

"What's happened?" Shanna repeated.

"I don't want to talk about it on the phone."

Jace rolled his eyes. He'd put his money on excitement. Apparently good old Dirk had seen a few too many spy movies.

Shanna gave him a quelling look. "Please, Dirk. You have to tell me what you heard."

"The government is involved. I overheard Mr. Barstow talking about a meeting with a government agent. He said it was all your fault."

"A government agent?" She met Jace's eyes and shook her head. "I don't see how I have anything to do with a government agent showing up."

Apparently she had about as much clue about what Dirk was babbling about as Jace did. "Is it the FBI, the IRS, what?" Jace asked. He was shooting in the dark. He had no idea why any federal agency would be involved. Murder was a state crime…providing that's all Shanna was wanted for.

He shoved that thought to the back of his mind. No use borrowing trouble. If he needed that worry, he knew where to find it.

"I don't know what agency. Barstow didn't say. Put Shanna back on."

"I'm on, Dirk. You can talk in front of Jace. Like I said, he's helping me." She looked straight at him, a warmth in her eyes that penetrated to the bone.

"Is Linda with you, too?"

"No."

"I wanted to tell you. This morning when I saw you at the door, I was responding to Linda's card. She was flagged as a security risk."

"A security risk? Why?"

"I don't know. Maybe the police wanted to talk to her."

Shanna shook her head. "She already talked to the police the day before."

"Maybe Mr. Barstow figured she'd try to help you. Whatever the reason, she might be in danger."

"She knows, Dirk. She's somewhere safe."

"So it's just you and this Jace?"

Jace wanted to roll his eyes again. Dirk sure had it bad for Shanna. He'd bet the behemoth would prefer he'd just walk away. Too bad that wasn't going to happen.

"Yes, Dirk. It's just me and Jace." She glanced at him.

All the heat of the afternoon suffused his body. If he didn't take his eyes off her, he'd be ready for action in more ways than one.

"I don't know, Shanna," Dirk whined over the phone. "You can't be too careful about who you trust. Not with uranium in the center of this."

Uranium. Jace managed to pull his focus from Shanna. What was the security guard implying? His pulse quickened. He'd been under the assumption they were dealing with raw uranium, nothing refined or even approaching weapons grade. Refined uranium was used for a host of things that could be considered sensitive. From nuclear power…to nuclear weapons.

Maybe Dirk was on to something. Maybe it wasn't the FBI. Maybe it was homeland security…the NSA…who knew? Maybe this thing was bigger than a fake mine. Maybe it was far bigger than they'd imagined.

Shanna let out a heavy sigh. "If only we had that laptop. Then we'd have something to give them."

Jace knew she hadn't meant the words to cut him, but he felt the slash all the same.

"Laptop?" Dirk's voice rose from the phone.

"Yeah," Shanna answered. "My laptop. It has copies of the accounts I was working on before I left for the hunting trip. Mr. Barstow took it from my apartment." She looked up at Jace and mouthed *not your fault.*

He wished that took away the sting. It wasn't even close.

"Mr. Barstow has it?"

Shanna nodded. "Yeah, why?"

"It's in his office. I saw it. He left it on the credenza. It's still there. I can get it. I can bring it to you."

Shanna drew in a shaky breath.

Jace wasn't sure her reaction was from distrust of Dirk or worry about him getting more deeply involved in something dangerous. From what he'd learned about Shanna over the past few days, he was betting on worry.

Good thing Jace wasn't about to look a gift horse in the mouth, as the saying went. "Do it, Dirk."

"Okay. I will. Where should I meet you?"

Shanna chewed on her bottom lip, as if she still wasn't so sure.

Jace didn't know Palmer as well as either of them, and hesitated to use the park again. He didn't want to become predictable.

"I'll meet you at the bus station."

Jace almost rolled his eyes. "The bus station? Are you crazy? That's one of the main places the police will be watching, waiting for Shanna to skip town."

"Sorry. I'm not very good at this."

At least he admitted it. "How about something more unexpected?"

"The high school. There's a game tonight."

That was a little more public than Jace had in mind. What if someone recognized Shanna and called the police? He shot her a questioning look.

She nodded. Holding the phone away from her ear, she cupped her hand over it so Dirk couldn't hear. "We can go in the back way. It will be dark. No one will see me well enough to recognize me. And you have to admit, it's the last place anyone would expect me to be."

Jace nodded.

She returned the phone to her ear. "Behind the concession stand."

Dirk's voice rose in an excited whisper, the last vestiges of his panic apparently washed away by the prospect of playing spy. "Perfect. The game starts at seven. I'll be there at eight."

"Good." Jace hit the off button. If he planned to arrive at

eight, Jace and Shanna would be there at seven-thirty and intercept him outside the gate.

Just because Jace trusted the guy enough to let him help didn't mean he was willing to bet Shanna's life and his own. The wire they were walking was high, and there was no way in hell Jace was going to let either of them fall.

SHANNA HUDDLED in the shadows behind the Palmer High bleachers and searched the crowd of proud parents and teenagers inside the chain-link fence. The heat she'd felt out on the prairie with Jace was only a memory, a memory she wanted to hold on to with all her might.

She could still feel the whisker burn on her cheeks and inner thighs. Still feel the power that had flowed through her when she'd taken control. She was sure her muscles were sore from all they'd done, too. But that pain merely blended with all the other aches she'd accumulated over the past days. Even though she was shaking again, from the cold, from the sharp edge of fear, she wasn't the same as before. She'd never be the same.

She just hoped those few moments had given both her and Jace enough to see them through whatever lay ahead.

Judging from the tension visible in the lines around Jace's eyes, he was feeling as edgy as she was. "Where the hell is he?"

"Are you sure we didn't miss him? What if he's already at the concession stand?"

"I'll take a walk over and see."

She shoved herself away from the frigid wire fence. "I'll go with you."

Following the fence, which skirted the back edge of the bleachers, they worked their way within sight of the concession stand. Parents stood in line for hot cocoa, coffee and popcorn. The scents tickled the cold air, reminding Shanna just how long it had been since she'd eaten. How long since she'd been able to do something as cozy as sip hot cocoa with Emily. How long it might be until she could do those things again.

If she could at all.

Jace grasped her hand and pulled her behind the corner of the last bleacher section.

"Did you see him?"

"No. He's not there." He checked his watch for what had to be the twentieth time. "Twenty minutes late now."

Shanna swallowed into a tight throat. "Something happened."

"You don't know that."

"Dirk is very punctual."

"Maybe he was delayed."

She searched Jace's face. "Do you really think that's probable? That he was delayed for some innocent, coincidental reason?"

She could tell by the look in his eyes that he didn't.

"Let's go." She spun around and started back the way they'd come, back to the spot where they'd left Dirk's car.

Jace grasped her arm. "Wait. We can't march into the Talbot building, if that's what you had in mind."

She had to admit, she didn't know what she had in mind. Something to help Dirk. Anything. She'd had so many misgivings when he'd volunteered to get the computer. So many horrible possibilities had raced through her mind. But she hadn't told him no. She'd pushed all her worries aside. She'd gone along with the plan, despite putting him in danger. She'd focused on how he could help her instead of how this could hurt him.

She had to make sure he was okay. "Ideas?"

"You know where he lives?"

She'd gone to a picnic at his house the summer before. He'd kept putting his arm around her, suggesting they were an item. She'd just sat there, uncomfortable, not knowing what to do, not wanting to hurt his feelings or make him angry. Somehow feeling as if the misunderstanding was all her fault. The memory was so distant, it seemed as if it had happened to another person. "I know where he lives."

"Then that's where we'll go."

Shanna took a deep breath and nodded. Dirk had to show up at home eventually. After the police were done questioning him. After Barstow handed him his pink slip on a plate. After the federal government... Oh, God, just let him show.

The drive didn't take long, not now that they had a car. Even so, by the time they parked at the end of the court and climbed from the car, Shanna's heart was beating so hard she could hardly hear Jace's whisper. "We'll circle around the back. That way we can see if he's home before he, or anyone else, sees us."

She forced a nod. What would she do without Jace? She hated to think.

They circled a planting of juniper and started crossing the first backyard. A light shone from the window. She could see a woman inside, her head bent over the sink, washing dishes. Funny that people were still going about their everyday routines, doing mundane chores, trying to find something to watch on television, even arguing with their spouse or children. None of them really knew how lucky they were. Or what was really important. Not until their worlds were turned upside down.

The sound of a door sliding cut the stillness. Shanna froze, not sure from which house the sound had come.

Jace brushed her arm. He pointed to the yard they were

about to enter. A tiny dog scampered out the door and started sniffing the grass. The dog might not pose much of a threat—at least not compared to the killing machine in the junkyard—but she bet it could make a racket.

Motioning to her, Jace changed direction, heading for the yard behind the little dog's. A three-foot fence separated the two properties. He stepped over the fence, then held out a hand for Shanna.

She grasped his hands and swung her leg over the fence.

The little dog let out a startled yap.

Shanna scrambled to gain footing on the other side. Damn, her legs. They were too short. She was too slow. She was too weak. She hadn't known how poorly she stacked up until the last few days.

Jace reached over the fence. He circled her rib cage with his hands and lifted. Gathering her into his arms, he carried her across the fence and set her down on the other side. They crouched down in the shadows.

She exchanged looks with him in the dark. Once again, he'd been there when she'd needed him. Once again he'd helped her deal with what she couldn't deal with alone.

Her throat grew thick. The whole thing was insignificant, stupid, really. They'd been through so much more than crossing a fence. Yet for some reason, it was all hitting her now. What in the world would she have done without him? Why in the world was he still sticking around?

She pushed the questions from her mind and focused on the roof of Dirk's house. Dirk, too, had been there to help her. And Linda. She owed all of them. But her thoughts kept winding their way back to Jace, causing her to feel strong one moment, vulnerable the next.

Maybe she was finally going out of her mind.

Crouching, Jace moved along the fence where the dog couldn't see them. Shanna followed, forcing herself to concentrate on the task at hand. The dog yapped a few more times, then was quiet. Reaching the far corner of the yard, Jace stopped. They peeked over the fence.

A light shone from Dirk's window.

A muffled sound, like a laugh, bubbled in Shanna's throat. She hadn't realized how frightened she was until just then.

He'd made it home. Thank God.

They climbed over the fence and entered the corner of Dirk's yard. More than anything, Shanna wanted to race across the yard, barge through the door and yell for Dirk, to make sure he was all right. Instead, she kept behind Jace, moving quietly and carefully across the yard and to the patio.

Edging up to the glass door, Jace peered inside.

Shanna forced herself to stay at his shoulder. "Do you see him?"

"No."

"He must be upstairs."

"Wait a second."

"What is it?"

Jace grasped the door handle. Unlocked, it slid open easily, silently. "Stay here." He slipped inside before Shanna could protest.

She entered right on his heels.

"Oh, God." Jace spun around. He grasped her shoulders and pushed her back toward the door. "I told you to stay outside."

Panic surged through her. She fought to break free from his hands, to see beyond the kitchen. She ducked to the side and ripped from Jace's grip.

She stumbled forward, half-expecting to see Dirk or the

sheriff or Barstow himself to be standing in the shadows with a gun.

What she saw was a dark shape sprawled on the floor of the family room…blood soaking into the carpet.

get un for some trouble if you hang around here any longer. I'm sure.

Maybe she was just nothing more than waiting for the tree of the no firefly room. I could pour the water out tonight.

# Chapter Sixteen

"Dirk!" She raced across the kitchen.

Dirk lay on his side, facing away from them. Red soaked into carpet fibers, spreading out from his back like an aurora.

She dropped to her knees. She grabbed his shoulder and pulled him onto his back.

His open eyes stared up at her. The pupils held a grayish cast. Blank. Dead.

Her chest squeezed. *No, no, no.* She couldn't think. She couldn't breathe.

Hands grasped her shoulders, Jace's hands. He started pulling her away.

She tried to shrug him off. "He can't be dead. He can't be."

"He is."

"No." She fought free of Jace's grip. She'd gotten Dirk involved in this. She'd put him in danger. He couldn't be dead. There had to be a way for her to save him.

She ripped his jacket open. Blood drenched his white uniform shirt. She had to do something. She tore the shirt open. A dark hole puckered in the center of his white chest.

She'd taken first aid years ago. Pressure. She had to put pressure on the wound. She had to stop the bleeding. She wadded up his jacket and held it against what appeared to be the source of the blood.

Again, Jace's strong hands clamped down on her shoulders. "He's not bleeding anymore, Shanna. His heart isn't pumping. He's dead."

She pressed a shaking hand to Dirk's throat, felt the soft glands under his jaw, felt the bulge of his Adam's apple, felt the threads of arteries under the skin. But she couldn't detect a pulse. Couldn't feel any stirring of life. His throat was oddly cool under her fingertips.

A surge of emotion stung behind her eyes. Tears gushed free and streamed down her face. "It's all my fault. All my fault."

"It's not."

"It is." She gasped in a breath. She never should have asked for his help. She should have refused when he offered. Dirk was a good man. And now he was dead because of her.

"Shanna, we've got to get out of here."

Something hit the toe of her boot. She looked down. Something had fallen from Dirk's jacket, which was still wadded in her hand. She blinked, straining to see through her tears.

A tiny key lay on the carpet, a bulbous orange plastic base encased the end. Shanna picked it up. She looked at it for a second on her open palm, but all she could focus on was Dirk's blood staining her skin.

A siren screamed outside.

"Come on, Shanna. Now!" Jace grabbed her arm and yanked her along behind him.

Stuffing the key in her pocket, she scrambled to keep up with him. "My laptop! Did you see my laptop?"

"No!" Jace barked. He dragged her out the door. They sprinted across the yard.

When they reached the fence, Shanna glanced behind. Red

and blue lights reflected off the house's eaves and pulsed in the night. Sirens ripped the air. The yaps of the dog next door hit her nerves like the strike of a ball-peen hammer.

Neighbors' lights flashed on all around.

They vaulted the fence and ran along the edge of the property. Shanna's head pounded. Her breath rasped in her ears. They reached the end of the yard, leaped the fence again and raced through another.

Where did they leave the car? Shanna wasn't sure. The only thing she knew was the police were behind them, that if they didn't find the car soon, they wouldn't have a chance of getting away. And that with all the blood on her hands and clothes, it wouldn't take much for them to conclude she'd murdered Dirk.

Maybe they were right. Maybe she had.

A jangle of shouts erupted behind them. This time Shanna didn't turn around. She kept her eyes on Jace's shoulders, kept her grip tight on his hand, and ran for all she was worth.

SHANNA STARED at the cable news report on the cabin's satellite TV. She'd turned the volume down, unable to listen to the anchor's speculation about what a horrible person she must be. Endless tears made her eyes burn. They ran hot down her cheeks. She wanted to change what had happened, erase what she'd seen. But it had finally sunk in that it was too late. "I never should have let him help."

Jace stopped pacing and turned to look at her. "That was his decision. Not yours."

"I could have told him no."

"Shanna…"

"I could have. Instead, I used him. I saved myself by sacrificing him." She rubbed her forehead with her fingertips, digging hard into her skin. "I get it now, what you said before about being desperate, about selling out anyone if the stakes are high enough."

"Forget what I said, Shanna."

"It was true. That's what I did. I sold Dirk out. I put him in danger to save my own skin."

"You didn't do anything of the kind." He sat down beside her on the love seat. Raising a hand, he ran his fingers along her cheekbone and through her hair. "He wanted to help you. He tried. What Barstow or the sheriff or whoever shot him did isn't your fault any more than Roger's or Davis's deaths were."

His touch was so tender, his words so caring, they only made Shanna want to cry harder.

A photo flashed on the screen. She blinked the tears back and tried to see it more clearly. In the grainy image, two people were running from a glass-doored building. It took her a moment, but she knew who it was and when it was taken. Her and Jace, escaping from the Talbot building early that morning.

Just when she thought things couldn't get worse. "They have your picture. I can see your face."

Jace narrowed his eyes on the TV. "Part of my face."

He was right. His hat shielded his eyes. Several days' growth of beard obscured his jawline. On the other hand, Shanna had forgotten to replace her sunglasses on her mad dash out of the building. The camera had gotten a clear shot of her, new hairstyle and all.

She read the scroll beneath the images. Her stomach hitched. "They think we killed Dirk." She'd known it was coming. Since they ran from Dirk's house, police lights flashing, she'd known his murder would be blamed on her and Jace. But seeing it on national cable news was almost more than she could take.

"At least they don't have a gun with your fingerprints on it this time."

Fingerprints. She hadn't even thought of that. "Did you touch anything in Dirk's house?"

Jace nodded, a matter-of-fact look in his eye. "The door. I tried to smear the prints on our way out, but there's no telling how successful I was."

"You were in prison."

"And on the police force. They have my prints on file. If any prints survived, they'll be able to trace them to me."

More tears wove their way down her cheeks and pooled under her chin. It just kept getting worse and worse. Now Jace would be pulled into this even deeper than he was already. Now his life would be ruined, too. "There has to be something we can do."

"There is."

"What?"

"The same thing we were trying to do before Dirk offered his help. Get our hands on that laptop."

Shanna frowned. She'd assumed her boss had taken it from Dirk when he'd shot the security guard. "You think Mr. Barstow doesn't have it?"

"I don't know. He might. But then, he might not." He nodded to the pocket of her jeans. "What did you pick up back there? What fell out of Dirk's coat?"

She dipped her hand in her pocket and pulled out the key.

Jace stared at it and shook his head. An incredulous smile spread over his lips. "I can't believe it."

"What?" Maybe her mind was still frozen from shock, but she wasn't following whatever it was that Jace found so obvious.

"Bus stations have lockers that use keys like that."

"You think he put my laptop in a locker at the bus station?"

He tilted his head to the side as if that was exactly what he thought. "It seems that Dirk was so enthralled with the thought of using the bus station to meet and exchange the laptop, he stashed it there anyway. Unless…"

"Unless what?"

"Unless he already had it before we talked to him. Did you mention the laptop when you asked to use his car?"

She searched her memory. "I think I did. What does that mean?"

"Probably nothing. Probably Dirk planned all along to win you over by delivering that laptop. Maybe the high school football game was another part of his fantasy. Reliving his glory years or finally getting the girl at the game like he'd never been able to do in high school. Who knows?"

Shanna stared at the key. She didn't know what Dirk planned. She wished he could be there to tell them in person.

"So you see? It wasn't your fault. Likely Dirk got the computer before he ever talked to you. And if he'd played it straight instead of trying to orchestrate some sort of heroic spy adventure or relive his high school days, he would have been able to give it to you right away. And maybe he wouldn't have gotten shot."

Shanna knew there was something to all the things Jace was saying, but it didn't change the one fact that mattered. Dirk died trying to help her. And she couldn't let something like that happen again. "I'm going to the bus station. If the laptop is there, I'm going to get it."

"Don't be ridiculous."

"My problem. My solution."

"Shanna, you just saw the news reports. The police will be on you before you find the locker."

She met Jace's eyes. "You were on television, too."

"Only part of my face. I won't be as easy to recognize."

"They have your fingerprints, Jace. We have to assume they do. And that part of your face might be enough."

"I'm willing to take the chance."

"I'm not."

Jace blew out a frustrated breath. "If not me, how about Linda? No one is looking for her."

Shanna's throat felt tight. Asking Linda to retrieve the laptop seemed like a logical choice, except...

She shook her head. All she could think about was Dirk's shirt, red with blood. All she could see was his flat, dead eyes. "I can't."

"Linda's your friend. She wants to help."

"Dirk wanted to help, too."

"Dirk's death isn't your fault. We've already established that."

She whirled on Jace. Her throat pinched. Her stomach cramped. The urge to hit something boiled in her blood. "How can you say that? He never would have been killed if he didn't try to help me. I shouldn't have let him. I signed and sealed his death sentence. Whether he took the laptop before we got back to Palmer or after doesn't make one damn bit of difference."

Jace stared at her, no longer arguing.

Of course, how could he argue? The cause of Dirk's death was obvious. "I'm not going to put Linda in that position. I'm not going to put you in that position, either. I'm going to get the computer myself."

Jace glanced at the television screen, then back to her. "You won't make it."

"At least I won't be putting someone else at risk." That, she couldn't stomach. Already she would never forgive herself.

"Let me do it."

What? Was he deaf? "You don't get it, do you?"

He gestured to the television. "I can change my appearance. I can slip through unrecognized."

"Absolutely not."

"It would work."

"It might not."

"Shanna, it's worth the risk to me." Jace covered her hand with his. "You're worth the risk."

She shut her eyes. She couldn't look at him, couldn't allow herself to hear his words or soak in the warmth of his touch. She pulled her hand away. "I can't."

"I'm already in this up to my neck."

"And I'm sorry about that."

"Nothing's going to happen."

"Stop."

"Think of Emily. Don't you want to return to her? Don't you want to end this?"

"Of course I do." Tears streamed down her cheeks, more tears than she ever thought she could cry. But she didn't care. She had no answers. No options. Her heart was breaking in two. She looked Jace straight in the eye. "Don't you understand? I care about you, Jace. More than I ever wanted to. More than I should. You've helped me so much already. You've given me someone to believe in, someone who's every bit as heroic as he seems. If something happened to you, I couldn't live with myself."

"Nothing's going to happen to me."

"Now you're the one who's in denial."

"Maybe. But at least I'm not giving up."

"That's not what I'm doing."

"It isn't?"

"No!"

"You'll be sacrificing yourself if you try to get that laptop."

"Better than selling out someone else." She dug her fingers

into her forehead, kneading it as if the pressure would help her think. If she'd been able to come up with another solution—a way to keep Jace from risking himself and still ensure that she could return to Emily—she would have jumped on it in a minute.

"I'm sorry I ever told you what happened with my partner."

"It doesn't matter whether you told me or not, Jace. I still wouldn't have let you risk yourself this way."

"That's not your decision to make."

She gripped the key hard in her fist. Sharp edges digging into her flesh, she stuffed it into her pocket. "Yes, it is."

JACE STARED AT SHANNA. He couldn't believe she was doing this. "I need a drink." He turned away from her and retreated into the kitchen before he gave in to his need to take her by the shoulders and shake her until her sense returned. Rummaging through the liquor cabinet, he located a bottle of Glenlivet. But instead of putting the bottle to his lips and drinking away his frustration, he leaned on the counter. He felt sick.

"Are you okay?"

He gritted his teeth. Even now she was concerned about him. Even now.

"I'll be fine." Grabbing the bottle, he strode for the bathroom and shut the door behind him.

He screwed off the cap on the booze and took a deep slug. The scotch burned down his throat, warming him from the inside out, but it did nothing to wipe the sick feeling away. He stared at his reflection in the bathroom mirror.

Damn Shanna. Damn her. How could she do this? How could she pull him into this mess, make him care about her, then shut him out? He knew she thought she was doing this to help him. To protect him. A reaction to his fears of her selling him out. A reaction to the danger Linda was in. A reaction to Dirk's death.

He set the bottle aside and leaned against the vanity. Damn, damn, damn. Why had he told her about what Darla had done? Why had he heaped all that on her head?

Because he was a selfish bastard, that's why.

He hadn't known Shanna then. Hadn't recognized what a giving woman she was. How positive and caring and... glowing. He hadn't realized the part of her that would never sell him out was the precise quality that drew him in the first place. It was the light he'd seen in her eyes when she'd first peered at him from the cab of his truck.

But not realizing was no excuse.

He'd been so worried about his own skin, so concerned with protecting himself from the disappointment—hell, the unadulterated load of crap—that Darla had brought down on his head, that he hadn't let himself see that Shanna was nothing like Darla.

Well, he got his wish, hadn't he? He was going to be sitting around this cabin safe and sound while Shanna charged into that damn bus station, risking her own life and her little girl's future.

Yesterday all he cared about was bringing Barstow and Gable down. So much had changed since then. He'd changed. This wasn't about Barstow and Gable anymore. It wasn't even about Roger and the other guy and Dirk.

He was in this for Shanna.

God help him, he was falling in love with her.

He picked up the bottle and brought it to his mouth, ready to drink himself into pitiful oblivion.

Unless...

He set the bottle back on the vanity.

Maybe he didn't have to sit back and let her take on this burden. If he could get that key...

He opened the mirror and started rummaging through the bottles in the medicine cabinet. He plucked a bottle from the shelf and read the dosage guidelines before prying open the cap. Yes, that would do. It was even in capsule form. He spilled a dose into his palm and slipped it in his pocket. He just needed one of those crystal tumblers from the wet bar.

He was about to close the cabinet when a pair of scissors and a razor caught his eye. He set them out on the countertop and located some shaving cream. Perfect.

Leaving the bathroom, he carried the bottle of scotch back to the living room.

Shanna still sat on the couch, arms wrapped around her chest, the key probably still in her pocket.

He held the bottle up and gave her a look he hoped she would read as apologetic. "I hate to drink alone. Want one? Just a splash? It'll take the edge off."

She gave a reluctant nod.

He doubted she wanted a drink at all. But he knew she'd do it to humor him. She couldn't turn down his peace offering. That damn sense of decency running through her was too strong for her to reject his bid to make amends.

He poured two tumblers of Glenlivet and spilled the sleeping pills into one.

Shanna would never forgive him, of that he was certain. But she'd have a shot, and so would Emily. He could give them that. And he had every intention of returning after his visit to the bus station so he could explain his reasons to her, face-to-face.

And if something should go wrong, at least this time laying his head on the chopping block was his own idea.

# *Chapter Seventeen*

Shanna struggled to open her eyes despite the pounding in her head. What had happened? She must have fallen asleep. The last thing she remembered was talking to Jace, drinking the scotch he'd poured for her, then deciding to take a little nap before leaving for the bus station.

Her eyes ached. Her lower lids were swollen from tears. Her head felt like fog punctuated by a splitting headache. She sat up on the love seat and looked around the cabin. She didn't hear Jace. Had he gone to bed?

She forced herself up on unsteady feet and walked through the kitchen. She climbed the stairs and checked the bedrooms. No Jace.

An uneasy feeling nipped at the back of her neck. Where could he be? The garage?

After they'd run from Dirk's house, they'd doubled back to the park along the river and left Dirk's car. There, they'd picked up their motorbikes from the spot they'd left them earlier in the day. One of the bikes was running a little rough. Could that be what Jace was up to? Fixing the bike?

She made her way back down the stairs and through the kitchen. Peeking her head into the garage, her unease turned to full-fledged alarm.

Not only was Jace nowhere to be found, but one of the motorbikes was also missing. Shanna slipped her hand into the pocket of her jeans.

Her fingers touched nothing but lint.

JACE INSERTED THE KEY into the bus-station locker. The mechanism turned with a click. Sucking in a breath, he pulled the door open and peered inside.

A black, zipped case filled the small space. Glancing over his shoulder in as blasé a way as he could muster, he pulled the case from the locker and let out the breath he'd been holding.

So far, so good.

He shrugged the strap over his shoulder and walked from the station. Approaching the door, he spotted the security camera staring down at him. A weary employee nodded to him from behind the ticket counter. A janitor didn't even look up from the floor he was mopping.

Jace pushed through the door and stepped into the cool dawn. The town was still, the air quiet. Even the birds were hushed, most either leaving or already left for warmer climes.

He wished he could join them. Him and Shanna and Emily.

He shivered and hiked the collar of his coat higher around his neck. What he wouldn't give for his hat right now. He had no idea how cold an autumn morning could be without his hat…or his hair.

Unable to resist, he raised his hand to his head and ran his fingers over his smooth scalp. Being bald was a little surreal. Though judging from the ease with which he'd slipped in and out of the bus station, it was plenty effective. Still, not a look he was eager to keep, that's for sure. At least he knew he could pull it off. Just in case it didn't grow back.

He ducked behind the Laundromat four doors down from

the bus station and pulled his motorbike from its hiding place. It had coughed and choked all the way into town. He hoped to hell it got him back to the cabin. He couldn't wait to hear Shanna's reaction to his new look.

That is, if she would talk to him at all after what he'd done.

SHANNA CHECKED the clock on the kitchen wall. By now, Jace either had the laptop or he didn't. If he'd managed to get it, and it contained evidence of Mr. Barstow's crime, everything would be over soon. If not, their last hope of proving Barstow's embezzlement was gone, as was her hope of clearing her name.

Either way, the outcome was no longer up to her. What she couldn't figure out was why she still felt so uneasy. If they'd found the answer, why did she sense she was missing something? Something big?

Maybe it had to do with what Dirk had suggested over the phone. That Mr. Barstow was into something larger. That a federal agency was involved.

She'd gone through everything she had, including the calendar pages from her office and her memories of the financials for the Hell's Half Acre mine, and even tried to recreate her past month at work to no avail. She was out of ideas.

She started gathering the few things she had at the cabin, her hunting clothes and personal items, and stuffing them into the plastic bags. Her legs trembled, a feeling she was getting far too used to lately. She'd have to talk to Jace about the federal-agency angle. She'd have to talk…

She leaned on the table. She didn't know what to think about Jace. She didn't know how to feel. When she'd noticed a motorbike and the bus-station key gone, she'd been angry. Now she was simply confused. He'd deceived her. Drugged her. And stolen the key.

She knew he'd done it for her. That he wanted to prevent her from being recognized. That he wanted to bring an end to this nightmare just as much as she did. But did the end justify the means?

She didn't know.

Legs trembling, she sank down on a dinette chair. She'd been through such a roller coaster of emotion in the past days, she wasn't sure she knew how to feel about anything. If this ever did end, she'd have to get far away from Jace before she decided anything. She'd let her emotions catch up. She'd let the fog of attraction clear. Then she'd decide if she could ever trust him again.

*If* they got out of this...

Linda was right. She saw what she wanted to see with men. Shanna had ended up being right about Dirk. He was a loyal friend. Whatever his motives, he'd tried to help. The rest didn't really matter. But had she been right about Jace? She'd thought so. Now she wasn't sure.

At least Emily was safe. And Linda. She couldn't wait to hug her friend. Linda had always been there for her, ever since Shanna had moved to Palmer. And what had Shanna done in return? Put her in danger. Jeopardized her job. Made her leave her home.

Guilt added to the unease bearing down on Shanna. She never should have talked Linda into letting her borrow her security card. Dirk had said it was flagged as a security risk. Now Mr. Barstow knew Linda was helping her.

She raised her hand to her shoulder, trying to massage away the tension running from her neck through her arm. The question was, how had Mr. Barstow known?

Linda had cooperated with the police at work that day. She'd cooperated later when they'd arrived at her condo. As far as Shanna knew, Linda didn't have a problem with police.

But she did have a problem at Talbot. There she was flagged as a security risk.

Scratch that. There *her card* was flagged as a security risk. But how had that happened? No one knew Shanna planned to use her card.

No one but Linda herself.

Shanna felt dizzy. Her face grew hot. There had to be another answer, another explanation.

She ran over events in her mind. Police had showed up at Linda's door shortly after she and Jace had arrived. Could be coincidence. Could be their junker truck and their circular route to her door had made neighbors suspicious.

But then Linda's card was flagged as a security risk when there was no reason for it, at least no reason she could quite believe.

And Dirk…oh, God, Dirk. No one had known Dirk was helping her. Not unless Dirk had given himself away. But Shanna had told Linda herself.

Pressure assaulted Shanna's chest, making it hard to breathe. Any one of those things could have another explanation. Any one of them could be coincidence.

But all of them together?

Panic bubbled hot under her skin. She started for the garage and the remaining motorbike inside.

Everything that Linda had helped her with had backfired. Everything she'd shared with Linda had made it back to Mr. Barstow. Maybe there was an innocent explanation. Maybe not. Shanna didn't know what was going on, but she knew one thing. Linda had Emily.

But not for long.

Shanna's hands were shaking when she reached Linda's mother's trailer, but it wasn't from the vibration of the bike. She was nervous. No, she was scared.

Linda knew how hard it would be for Shanna to stay away from Emily for any length of time, so her friend shouldn't be suspicious at her sudden appearance. The problem was getting Emily out of the trailer and on the dirt bike. Linda was smart. She would catch on fast.

She knocked on the trailer's aluminum storm door.

A shadow blocked the window. The door opened and Linda peeked her head through. "Shanna. Come on in." She stepped aside, ushering Shanna onto the worn linoleum.

The trailer smelled of stale smoke and pine cleaner. A sagging couch sat on one side of the small room, a round table and chairs on the other. Wood-print countertops and cabinets lined the back of the space, forming the kitchen.

"Mommy!" Her four-year-old raced across the uneven floor and threw herself into Shanna's arms.

Shanna knelt down and held her little body close. She inhaled the scent of crayons and graham crackers. It was all she could do to hold her ground and not just grab her baby and run.

"Where's the cowboy?" Linda looked down at her, hands on her fashionable hips.

For a woman who worked with money, Shanna had been utterly blind. Linda didn't make nearly enough to afford her fancy condo and closet of designer clothes. If Shanna hadn't been so desperate for a friend, she would have seen that. She would have wondered. "Jace left. We had a…falling out."

"What happened?"

"You were right. He wasn't the man I thought he was. Or at least not the man I wanted him to be."

"Jace?" Emily pulled her head from Shanna's shoulder and looked into her eyes. "Jace is like the red Power Ranger. Jace is a hero."

"Sure he is, sweetie." She patted her daughter's back and glanced around the trailer. Linda's mother must not be home.

Linda crossed her ankles and leaned against the kitchen counter. "I heard about the security guard on the news."

Shanna's stomach spun. She could still see Dirk's eyes, still smell the fleshy scent of his blood, still feel it sticky on her hands.

"They're saying you killed him."

She might as well have. "I didn't."

"They're saying you did. They're looking for you. Maybe even more than before."

"Listen, Linda. Can I have a moment with Emily? I just want to be with her alone."

Linda pursed her lips as if she wasn't quite sure.

Shanna's pulse thrummed in her ears. She tried to keep her breathing even. She tried to look at Linda just as she had before...before she suspected.

"I don't know if that's a good idea."

Shanna's stomach clenched. She couldn't tell if Linda's hesitation was due to worry that Shanna was a murderer or if she'd caught on that Shanna planned to take Em and run. She decided she'd play it as if it was the former...and pray it wasn't the latter. "She's my daughter, Linda. I'm not going to hurt her."

Linda gave a disapproving frown. "This whole mess is hurting her."

"I know. That's why I need to talk to her. Explain things."

"Maybe you should explain things to me, too."

"I will. After I talk to Em." She gave Linda a smile. Despite her best efforts, she could feel the corners of her mouth tremble.

Linda pushed her back up from the counter and opened a drawer. She started plunking silverware into it from the dish rack flanking the sink.

Shanna rolled her lips inward, hoping Linda hadn't noticed

the tremble. She had to get Emily out of here, and she had to do it now. She couldn't keep up the act. Linda knew her too well. "Em and I will go outside. We'll just be a few minutes. Then I'll explain everything to you."

Linda looked up. "No, I think you'll explain everything to me now." She lifted her hand from the drawer. In it she held a dull gray pistol.

Shanna's heart lurched into her throat. She glanced down at Em, then back to the woman she'd once thought was her friend. "Linda, you can't—"

"Oh, yes, I can." She held the gun steady and reached for her cell phone with the other hand.

Shanna stared into the black eye of the gun's barrel. She had the feeling she knew just who Linda was about to call.

# *Chapter Eighteen*

"Why did you do it, Shanna?" Linda had ordered her and Emily to sit on the couch. Now she sat in a chair ten feet away. Arms braced on the tabletop, she kept the gun pointed at Shanna's chest.

And waited.

Shanna looked her friend square in the eye. "I didn't do anything, Linda. Mr. Barstow did."

"You already did that song and dance."

"It's true." Shanna swallowed into a dry throat. Linda couldn't know everything that was going on. Shanna was sure she didn't. Otherwise she wouldn't go along. She couldn't do this. Not to Shanna. And certainly not to Emily.

The only chance Shanna had to get herself and her daughter out of this mess was to tell Linda the truth, all she knew of it, and hope her friend would believe her. "Mr. Barstow is embezzling from Talbot."

Linda arched her eyebrows. "Embezzling? I think not. Anthony built the company. He would protect it with his life."

Anthony. Not Mr. Barstow. Shanna didn't have to think too hard to know what Linda's name choice meant. She and Mr. Barstow had a relationship. A personal one. "Well, he's not protecting the company. He's stealing from it. You know the mine out near Hell's Half Acre? It doesn't exist."

Linda frowned.

"Jace and I went out there. We saw it. There's nothing there, Linda. Nothing but bare ground. Yet the financials say Heritage Mining, the company that owns it, is drowning in debt. It has all the debt of a very unsuccessful, working mine, yet it doesn't really exist at all. Except to suck money out of Talbot."

Linda didn't look impressed. "And to you that's evidence of embezzlement?"

"I haven't been able to find out who owns Heritage Mining. Not yet. But I have a feeling it's Mr. Barstow."

"You must think I'm awfully stupid. Anthony doesn't own Heritage. Talbot does. How can Talbot be embezzling from itself? But then you knew that, didn't you?"

Shanna leaned back on the couch. What was Linda saying? "No. I didn't know that. I didn't know any of it."

"You worked on the financials for the mine."

"You mean, the mine that doesn't exist?"

She waved a hand, as if that was a detail that didn't really matter. "You filed a report recommending Talbot close the mine. You knew exactly how much red ink was involved."

Linda's meaning dawned on her. She gasped for breath, feeling as if she'd just had the wind knocked out of her. "Heritage Mining. It's not a way for Mr. Barstow to embezzle money. It's a place for him to dump extra debt. To get it off Talbot's books."

Linda shrugged a shoulder. "No kidding."

Why hadn't she seen it before? If only she'd noticed the warning signs. If only she'd thought to do an overview of the whole company's financials when she'd noticed Heritage's debt. "So Mr. Barstow is diverting expenses and losses to

Heritage and then pretending it's a totally separate company from Talbot?"

"He's saving the company."

Saving the company? Who was Linda kidding? "Talbot is going bankrupt. Only no one knows it yet."

"Not once he can get the mill up and running. Anthony's buying time. The income from the mill will put the company back on firm footing. What he's doing is saving the company."

"Linda, I'll bet if you check, you'll see that Mr. Barstow has been dumping his stock as quickly as he can." She felt numb. Mr. Barstow wasn't the only one with significant money invested in Talbot. Most Talbot employees had their retirement funds wrapped up in company stock. Including her. Heck, most of Palmer had jumped on the bandwagon in anticipation of the coming uranium boom. "People are going to lose their life's savings."

Linda scoffed. "You act like you're so clean and pure. But I'll bet you sold your Talbot stock before you set up your meeting with the SEC."

"The SEC?" Shanna parroted. Her mind raced.

"You didn't think I knew?"

"My meeting with the SEC didn't have anything to do with you."

"Didn't have anything to do with me? Are you kidding? I have more than a 401K in Talbot. That company is everything I have. It's everything the town of Palmer has. But you didn't think about that, did you? You didn't think about anything but yourself."

"What are you talking about?"

"You. Destroying my livelihood. The whole town's livelihood. Just so you can be the perfect little Girl Scout."

She could see it now. She'd been invited on the hunting trip after her visit from the SEC. Linda must have reported it to

Mr. Barstow. "My meeting with the SEC agent had nothing to do with Talbot."

"And you expect me to believe that?"

"It was because of my ex-husband. I told you what he did. They're still investigating him."

Linda shook her head, as if the scenario she'd invented was so real to her it was all the proof she needed. "You were going to bring Talbot down. You were going to bring me down. Anthony was right to do what he did. He didn't have any other choice."

"Linda, Mr. Barstow murdered three people."

She shook her head. "That wasn't supposed to happen. That was all your fault. It was supposed to be a quick shot. Just you. A hunting accident. Then it was going to be all over."

"You knew about this from the beginning?"

A car door slammed outside.

"No. I didn't know about it. Not before you went on the trip. But Anthony explained it to me after. He was watching out for me. He was watching out for everyone at Talbot."

The door to the trailer rattled.

Linda smiled and moved to open it. "You were so set on bringing us all down? Well, now you're going to pay."

JACE WILLED the motorbike to make it up the swell in the mountain road. It coughed. It choked. It died again.

Damn.

He climbed off the bike and took another look. Hell if he knew what was wrong with it. He'd even put gas in it before he'd left town, thinking it might be low, but that hadn't changed anything.

He should have learned more about fixing engines when he was a teen.

He missed Dirk's car, not that they could have kept it. Not a good idea, driving a dead man's car. Especially when you're wanted for killing him.

Jace gave the bike a little twist of gas and tried to start it. It took on the third try, resuming its coughing and choking the rest of the way to the cabin.

At least he'd made it.

He swung his leg off the bike, careful of the laptop. He was looking forward to plopping this baby in front of Shanna. She might be angry. She might even hate him. He could live with all that. As long as they could find the answers they needed and end the danger she was in, he could live with just about anything.

He opened the small garage door and wheeled the bike inside. He paused at the spot the bikes were parked and blinked, trying to get his eyes to adjust to the dimness inside. But the problem wasn't his sight. It was the other motorbike.

Shanna was gone.

MR. BARSTOW'S broad shoulders and Armani suit looked out of place in the cramped quarters of the run-down trailer. When he'd arrived, he'd taken the gun from Linda and held it on Shanna while Linda tied her hands and feet. Then he'd ordered Linda to take the little girl into the next room so he and Shanna could talk.

Letting Emily go was the hardest thing Shanna ever had to do.

Barstow set the gun on the table. Placing a palm on either side of it, he leaned forward and stared at her with his probing blue eyes. The overhead light gleamed off his bald spot. "Dirk Simon took something from my office, Shanna. I want it back."

"I don't know what you're talking about. If he took something, I sure don't have it."

"You don't fool me, Shanna. You never have."

"That's funny. You sure fooled me. I thought you were a decent person."

"I am. To those who treat me decently. Isn't that right, Linda?"

Linda leaned in the corner, her arms crossed in front of her, pulling in. As though if she made herself small enough, she would disappear. "Just give him what he wants, Shanna. He's going to get it anyway. You can't win."

Shanna felt the bile rise in the back of her throat. Barstow made her sick, but seeing Linda cower to his will was worse. Shanna didn't know why she hadn't seen it before. "So let me guess. You two are having an affair."

Linda pushed up from the wall and slipped into the bedroom where she'd locked Emily, leaving Shanna alone with the boss.

"I'm disappointed in you, Shanna." Mr. Barstow's expression didn't change. He looked so calm, as if this was any other business meeting, just a little rebuke for a wayward employee. "I didn't want any of this to happen. You're the one who forced it. All I wanted was a little more time. Time to save my company, put it back on its feet. There are a lot of people relying on jobs Talbot provides. Hell, the whole town wouldn't exist if not for my company. You're the one who threatened to destroy it. You're the one who wanted to take it all away."

Shanna said nothing. Let him blame her for all the ills of the world. She didn't care. As long as she took all the blame he had to give, maybe he would just call the police and have them put her in jail. At least then Em would be safe.

But she feared that wasn't what he had in mind.

"Maybe your friend has the computer."

Shanna's chest tightened. Jace should make it back to the cabin soon. When he discovered her gone, he'd come looking for her. But he'd never find this trailer. She hadn't told him where it was.

"Where's the guy who was with you at the office? Cowboy hat?"

"I don't know."

"I think you do."

"I don't. I swear. He left sometime this morning."

"Left from where?"

She shook her head. She couldn't tell him about the cabin. What if Jace was already back? Once he had the laptop, she knew he'd return.

"Shanna, I don't want to ask you again."

"I already told you. I don't know."

He shook his head. "If you think I'm going to risk having some cowboy muddling things up after all I've been through, you sure didn't learn anything in your time working for Talbot."

She looked down at her feet.

"Okay, if that's the way you want to do it." He stood up from his chair.

She braced herself. She didn't know what he was planning, but she wouldn't be surprised if it involved pain. Mr. Barstow might seem calm on the outside, but there was something brutal about him. An energy. A scent in the air. Of course, she'd seen firsthand what he was capable of. She tried not to flinch as he stepped toward her.

He passed the couch she was sitting on and disappeared into the bedroom.

*Oh, God.* Fear ripped through her. Mind-numbing panic.

He emerged, holding Emily by the hand.

Shanna looked into her daughter's frightened eyes and started to shake.

"Okay, Shanna, let's try this again. Where can I find the cowboy?" He pointed the gun at Emily's head.

# Chapter Nineteen

Jace stared down at the blinking cursor on the laptop's screen. Time ticked by, and Shanna still hadn't shown. All their supplies were still here. Even her wallet was spread out on the kitchen table, along with the calendar pages from her office. She'd left in a hurry, but why? Where? The only place he could think that she might go was to Linda's mother's trailer to see Emily.

Too bad he had no clue where that was.

He focused on the cursor. It blinked impatiently, waiting for him to type in Shanna's password. He'd tried everything he could think of. None of it had worked. He finally had the laptop, right here in front of him, but he couldn't open the damn files.

Without Shanna, he was worthless.

He shoved his chair back from the table and thrust himself to his feet. He set out across the floor, pacing the same groove he'd walked for the past hour. He couldn't stand being so out of control. He couldn't stand being so helpless.

He couldn't stand not knowing where Shanna was, if she was okay, if she was even alive.

He hadn't known her long. Hell, only four days. Could it have been so little time? He felt as if he'd known her much longer. He felt like he'd known her forever. Maybe he'd just been waiting for her all these years.

She'd changed his life, that was for sure. And not just because of the predicament they were in. She'd changed who he was in more important ways than that. She'd opened him up. She'd made him stretch. She'd given him reason to hope.

He paced to the window and peered through spires of pine and fir. Since they'd found this place, it had felt like they were all alone. Deep in the wilderness. But that wasn't exactly the case. From the window he could see smoke rising from the cabin next door. A hunter walked toward him in the forest below.

Not a hunter.

Jace jolted back from the window. It was doubtful the man saw him. He was still too far away, and it was darker inside the cabin than outside in the bright sun. But Jace didn't want to take a chance. He had a feeling he knew the man outside. Judging from the way he walked, the way he held his rifle, his silver belly hat. He was no hunter.

He was Sheriff Benson Gable.

Jace closed his eyes. He wasn't one to believe in coincidences. And he was fairly certain no one had spotted him and Shanna and turned them in. That left only one person who could have told him about the cabin.

Shanna.

Pain ripped through him, followed by worry. Jace knew Shanna. She wouldn't sell him out. Even when he'd wanted her to let him take the risk of going to the bus station, she'd refused. She'd insisted on assuming all the risk herself. But there was one person she wouldn't risk. One person she'd do anything to protect. Including sacrificing herself. Including sacrificing him.

*Oh, Shanna, what happened? Where are you?*

He turned back to the window. He had to focus. He had to think.

Sheriff Gable found the cabin, but he didn't have Jace yet. And if Jace had anything to say about it, the sheriff's job was going to be a lot tougher than he thought.

He pulled back from the window. Hurrying, he crossed the kitchen and went into the garage. He scanned the space, looking for something he could use. A hunting rifle would be nice, but apparently that was too much to ask. His gaze landed on a shovel.

He grabbed it. It wasn't fancy, but with the element of surprise, it just might work. He opened the side door and slipped outside.

He plunged into the young forest of lodgepole pine. He moved quickly through the sparse understory. He had to be careful. With few bushes to hide behind, he had to take pains to keep Gable from spotting him. The man was a hunter, probably good at making his way over rocks and difficult terrain. But that didn't mean Jace wasn't better. Gable might think he was hunting Jace, but soon he would learn he was wrong.

Jace was hunting him.

There was one thing that confused him. The sheriff was approaching from the direction of the other cabin. Why? It would have been a lot easier for him to park directly in front of the cabin Jace was in. Not just easier, but quicker, stealthier. He could have stormed the door before Jace even knew he was outside.

Instead he must have parked at the cabin next door. Then made his way through the woods, poking around as though he was feeling his way in the dark. As if he was mistaken about exactly which cabin Jace was in.

Hot damn.

Shanna might have sold him out on the surface, but she'd left him some wiggle room. She'd sent Gable to the wrong cabin, the cabin next door. Jace could see it now. If things went badly and Gable caught him, she could just say she'd been confused. At the same time, by making Gable go out of his way, she increased the chance that Jace would notice the man. She'd given him a fighting chance.

And he was going to grab it with both hands.

He made his way up the slope. There. There was his spot. A fallen tree. A tangle of fir struggling to gain ground against the tall, straight pine. Rock sloped sharply down on the side Gable was approaching. Unless he wanted to walk a wide circle, he had to cross this spot.

Jace slipped behind the cover. Adrenaline coursed through his body, making him feel strong, making his senses sharp. He could hear Gable approach. The sheriff's footfalls were quiet, but definitely there.

One more step. Then another.

Jace tensed. The shovel handle felt slick in his hands. He gripped it harder. Waiting. Waiting.

The sound of the sheriff's breathing grew close.

*Now.*

Jace brought the shovel up. It caught the sheriff under the chin, sending him sprawling backward. Jace sprang to his feet and pounced. He jammed his forearm against Gable's windpipe. He grabbed the man's arm and flipped him onto his belly. He twisted the arm behind his back.

Gable grunted, stunned from the blow to his chin. Blood ran in a slash across his jaw.

Jace found the man's handcuffs. He slapped them on the wrist he was holding. Stretching Gable's other arm around the thin trunk of a pine, he clasped the cuff on the other wrist. He pulled the man's keys from his pocket.

"What the hell?" Gable shook his head and groaned. His eyes narrowed on Jace. His brows dipped in a deep frown as recognition dawned. "You."

Jace leaned over Gable, getting right in his face. "Where's Shanna Clarke?"

"You should have stayed out of this, son."

Anger fired in his blood. "You should have put your hand in your pocket instead of sticking it out for Barstow's cash. You should have done the damn job."

The man had the audacity to smile. "You want to know where to find her?"

"Where?"

"First, let me go."

What did Gable think he was? Stupid? "Like hell. Where is she?"

"I don't know where she is. I just know where she's going."

"And where is that?" Jace placed his knee in the middle of Gable's thigh. He leaned forward, his weight bearing down on the man's leg.

The sheriff's face turned red. He grunted in pain.

Jace let up before he broke the guy's femur. He wanted to see him in prison, not the hospital. An example of selling the law and paying the price. A lesson for law enforcement everywhere. "Where is Barstow taking her?"

A chuckle bubbled low in the sheriff's throat. "Shanna Clarke is going to hell. When you get there, say hi to her for me, would ya?"

Jace gave him a shove, then pushed himself away. Red crowded the edges of his vision. His hands ached to wrap themselves around Gable's neck and choke the laugh out of him.

He turned and started pacing. If he didn't get away from the man, he was going to do something he'd regret. Gable wasn't going to tell him anything. Not anything of value. He knew who buttered his bread. And he knew if Barstow succeeded in destroying the evidence against him, no one would touch him. Hell, they could probably blame the nonexistent mine on Shanna and get away with that, as well.

Jace had to think.

Gable's joke teased at the back of his mind. Hell? The sheriff didn't strike Jace as a religious man. Not that his actions had any bearing on that. *Anyone* could find a justification for doing *anything*. Religious people were just more creative than most.

Still, the way he laughed at his own joke suggested there was more to it. Particularly since the joke wasn't very funny.

A shiver like an electric charge traveled up Jace's spine.

Shanna was going to hell? Jace doubted it. But he had a feeling he knew were Barstow *was* taking her.

# *Chapter Twenty*

"See those cliffs?" Mr. Barstow lifted the barrel of his rifle, using it to point to a spot where the sharp edge of the canyon sliced into the sage-covered plain. "Native Americans used to herd bison off that drop. The animals would fall to their deaths on the rock below. A mass slaughter. You can still find bones at the bottom of the canyon."

Shanna gripped Emily's hand and stepped back, closer to the SUV. From this angle, she couldn't see the sheer drop to the craggy red, yellow and gray rock formations below. Fine with her. She didn't intend to get close enough to the edge to reenact Mr. Barstow's morbid history lesson. She had to find a way out before things got that far.

At least Barstow had agreed to untie her. Of course, she knew he hadn't done it so she could hold Em's hand. He'd wanted her to be able to walk to the cliff, to carry her daughter along, if need be. He probably figured with both he and Linda armed, there wasn't much Shanna could do.

She needed to find a way to prove him wrong.

"Let's take a walk." Barstow nodded to Linda.

The woman Shanna had thought was her friend stepped up beside her. She averted her eyes, waving her pistol to motion Shanna and Emily away from the SUV.

Shanna shivered despite the afternoon sun beating down on them. It seemed like ages ago that she and Jace had made love close to this very spot. Then the heat had felt delicious, the sweat covering her body incredibly sensuous, the wide-open sky freeing and empowering. Now even the sun seemed like her enemy, beating down, a glaring spotlight on the horrors to come.

She glanced at Linda. As betrayed as Shanna felt by her friend, she still couldn't believe Linda had it in her to help Barstow commit murder. If she could somehow reach Linda, cut through her rationalizations, make her recognize what was going on, what was about to happen…

"Lin?" she whispered, praying Barstow wouldn't hear. "Don't do this. Not to Em."

Linda kept her eyes focused on the canyon.

"Don't let Barstow hurt her, Lin. She's just a little girl. Please." She squeezed her daughter's hand.

Linda gave her head a little shake. "He's not going to. He promised."

"And you believe him?"

Linda raised her chin.

There had to be a way to reach her. A way to make her realize what she was doing. Linda prided herself on being logical. "Emily isn't a baby, Lin. She's not going to witness something and not remember."

Linda looked straight ahead. "Be quiet."

"I can't be quiet. I can't just go along. You can't, either."

"I said shut up."

She had no idea if she was getting to her friend or not. But she wasn't about to stop trying. Not when each step was bringing them closer and closer to the canyon. "I know you didn't mean for any of this to happen, Linda."

Linda didn't respond.

"How did it start? With him buying you things? Clothes? Jewelry?"

"He didn't buy me."

Shanna bit her lip. What was it then? She needed a way past Linda's defenses. She had to think.

Linda had grown up in a trailer, with a hopelessly alcoholic mother. Crushing poverty. Always wanting something better. In that way, Linda wasn't unlike Shanna. Shanna's mother hadn't been a drinker, but the three jobs she'd had to work to make ends meet after the divorce took their toll on any kind of home life.

She and Linda's common dream of a better life was one of the reasons they were friends. That and, she supposed, the scars left by fathers who'd disappeared from their lives when they both were young. And Shanna knew the one thing she herself had always responded to in a man. The thing that had always made her want to look past a man's faults. "He made you feel special."

Linda's stride faltered.

"Oh, Linda, you are special. You don't need him for that."

"I know what you're doing," Linda growled. "You're trying to wreck this for me."

"Linda, you can't just sit back and let him do this. He's going to kill us."

"You don't get it. Without him, I have nothing. I'm nobody. I'm sorry, Shanna. I really am. But it's either you or me."

Tears burned Shanna's eyes. She didn't want to believe Linda thought so little of herself. She didn't want to believe her friend only felt she had worth if she saw it reflected in Barstow's eyes.

She couldn't help thinking of Jace. He'd made her feel special, too. But it was so much more than that. He'd made her feel smart. Confident. Powerful. And most important, she'd always known those qualities were coming from inside her. That if he suddenly disappeared, her strength wouldn't go with him. That no matter what happened, those things that made her special were hers to keep.

How tragic that Linda didn't have that. How tragic that Shanna and Emily would have to pay the price.

"What are you girls talking about?" Barstow's voice boomed from behind them.

Linda raised her chin. "Nothing important. I was just setting Shanna straight."

"Good girl."

Shanna ground her teeth together. Coming from Barstow, it sounded like praise for a loyal dog.

Barstow circled around and stopped in front of them. They were close to the canyon now. Too close.

Shanna held on to Emily's shoulders. She shot Linda one last pleading look.

Barstow stepped up beside her. "Okay. Enough of this. Why don't we get this over with?" He grabbed her arm and wrenched her hands from Emily.

"Mommy!"

"Take the girl," he shouted to Linda.

Linda grabbed Em. Tears rolled down Em's little cheeks and gurgled in her throat with each scream. "Mommy!"

"It's okay, baby. Linda will take care of you. Everything will be all right." She gave Linda a pointed look, hoping beyond hope that her friend would find it inside her to fulfill the promise Shanna had just made.

Emily continued to scream, not hearing. Or maybe just not believing her assurances.

Mr. Barstow pulled her by the arm, closer and closer to the edge of the canyon. "I'm sorry I have to do this, Shanna. I sincerely wish there had been another way."

Yeah, right. She struggled to break free of his grip. At least she didn't have to make it easy. Despite her efforts, the canyon's edge loomed closer and closer.

Something caught her eye. A movement along the canyon's lip.

*A sheriff's coat and silver belly hat.*

A sob clogged her throat. It was over. All over.

Barstow shoved her.

She twisted her body to the side, stopping her momentum before she went over the edge. She sprawled headfirst into a clump of sage and clung.

"Gable?" Mr. Barstow called. "What the hell you doing down there?"

The man looked up.

Not Sheriff Gable. Jace. *It was Jace.*

Barstow brought the rifle to his shoulder.

Shanna scrambled to her knees, to her feet. She threw herself at Barstow. She plowed into his side. She reached her hands up, clawing at his face.

A crack split the air.

Cursing, Barstow regained his balance. He raised a fist and brought it down on her shoulder.

The force of his blow shot down her back and arm. She held on. She couldn't let him shoot Jace. She wouldn't let him kill Emily.

Barstow's fist came down on her a second time.

One hand slipped. She couldn't hold on.

He hit her again.

She fell to the ground. Air exploded from her lungs. She gasped for breath. Dust filled her throat, making her choke.

Barstow traced the edge of the cliff with the rifle's scope. "Dammit." He lowered the weapon and sneered down at

Shanna. He raised a foot and brought his steel-toed boot hard into her ribs.

"Mommy, Mommy, Mommy!"

Emily's shrill scream ripped through the pain fogging Shanna's mind.

"Shut her up," Barstow barked at Linda. He turned back to the canyon, leaving Shanna in an aching heap on the ground. "Okay, cowboy. Come on out here right now."

There was no sign of movement.

"I said right now, unless you want two deaths on your conscience."

Shanna looked up from the ground and met Linda's eyes. Emily wriggled in her grasp. Linda looked away.

"Okay, have it your way," Barstow's voice rang out over Hell's Half Acre. "Linda? Shoot the girl."

From where Shanna lay, she could see Linda's face go even whiter. "Please, Linda. No," she begged, her voice croaking through the dust.

"Do it," Barstow said. He scanned the canyon with narrowed eyes. "I'm not messing around with this crap anymore."

Shanna pulled in a breath. Her ribs screamed, but she didn't care. All she could think about was Emily. All she cared about was making her friend see what was happening before it was too late. "Please, Lin."

Mr. Barstow's boot lashed into her again.

Agony doubled her over. Darkness narrowed her vision. She lifted her head. She had to see Em. She had to reach Lin.

Linda's gaze focused on Shanna. She raised her chin, then she looked at Barstow. "You said Emily wouldn't get hurt. You promised me."

"Do it."

Linda paused. She scooped in a deep breath and wrapped her arms tight around Emily's tummy. *"No."*

## *Chapter Twenty-One*

Jace skirted the edge of the canyon, keeping low enough so he wouldn't be spotted from above. When he'd arrived at Hell's Half Acre in the sheriff's SUV and seen Barstow marching Shanna and Emily toward the cliff, he hadn't thought about anything but saving them. He'd panicked and rushed in like a damn amateur. If it wasn't for Shanna jumping Barstow, he'd be dead right now.

He had to play this smarter. He had to think. If he got close enough, he could rush Barstow. He could reach the bastard before he had the chance to level his rifle on any of them.

Voices rode the wind. Angry. Urgent.

Jace tried to breathe. His foot slipped. Rock clattered down the craggy cliff and dropped to the canyon floor.

He held his breath, waiting for Barstow to appear above him. Waiting for the bullet.

It didn't come.

Barstow must not have heard. Shanna must be keeping him too busy to notice.

He hoped to hell she wasn't getting herself hurt.

Jace kept moving along the edge. He had to get closer. A few seconds were all he had. He needed to be on Barstow before the man knew he was there. He couldn't charge in like a buffalo. If he got himself killed, he wouldn't be able to save anyone.

A shrill scream pierced the air.

Emily. Oh, God. He couldn't be too late. God, don't let him be too late.

He kept moving. Closer. Closer.

He could see Barstow's legs now. Dark trousers. A dusty pair of boots that probably cost as much as Shanna made in a month. The man was looking the other way.

Jace got into position. He secured his footing, ready to spring. He rose slowly, watching Barstow.

Shanna lay at his feet, curled into the fetal position, hugging her middle. She spotted him. Her eyes grew wide.

Gritting her teeth, she hoisted herself up in one motion. She slammed her fist into Barstow's groin.

Barstow bellowed. He brought the rifle down, trying to get a bead on Shanna.

Too late.

Jace plowed into him from behind. He kept his legs driving like a fullback.

The gun went off.

Jace braced himself for the slug's impact. The shot went wild.

He grabbed the rifle. He shoved a knee into Barstow's gut and wrenched the weapon from the CEO's hands. "You can't buy your way out of this one, you bastard." He plowed a fist into Barstow's jaw.

Barstow staggered back.

Jace brought the rifle around. He leveled it on the man.

Barstow spun. His boot skidded. He went down. He took one last lunge, trying to right himself....

And fell over the cliff's edge.

JACE RACED DOWN the hospital corridor as fast as his boots could take him across freshly waxed tile. He hoped to hell he wasn't too late. It had taken him far longer to reach the hospital in Jackson than he'd thought. He should have left his ranch earlier, but he'd had so much to do to get ready, he'd barely fit it all in.

But now he was here. Now he had everything prepared. All he needed was Shanna and Emily.

He reached the room number the woman at the front desk had given him. Gut as jittery as a high school boy at prom, he stepped through the door.

Empty.

Damn. Where could she be?

Had he missed her in the elevator? Had they crossed in some kind of parallel hallway?

He made his way back down the hall. He'd only been able to talk to her in snatches on the phone since he'd rushed her to the hospital after Barstow had fallen into the Hell's Half Acre canyon. Enough for her to explain the shell game Barstow had played with Talbot. Enough for her to tell him her mother was coming from St. Louis. That she'd take care of Emily for the couple of days the doctor insisted Shanna stay in the hospital. But her mother had to be back at work tomorrow. He sure hoped she hadn't taken Shanna and Emily with her.

He bounded down the stairwell to the first floor, not wanting to waste a second waiting for the elevator. He spotted a woman in a wheelchair near the front window. On her lap sat a little girl.

"Shanna."

She turned carefully toward him. A smile lit her bruised face.

A thickness lodged in his throat. She was so beautiful. So

strong. So alive. She had to listen to his idea. He could only pray she'd like what he had in mind.

"Jace!" Emily sprang off Shanna's lap and raced to him. She flung her little body into his arms.

He scooped her up into his arms and hugged her close, taking a long, slow breath of strawberry Jell-O and little girl.

She looked up at him, her big green eyes bright and shining, so like her mother's. "Do you have your Ranger?" She brandished her plastic woman, the pink one this time.

Jace dipped his hand in to the pocket of his coat and pulled out his red plastic man. "I sure do." He held it up for Emily.

She beamed. "Let's play!"

He braced her on his hip and looked into her little face. "We'll do that. But right now, I need to talk to your mommy about something. Something important."

"But I want to play Rangers."

"We will. I promise."

Her mouth turned down.

God, she was cute. And if Shanna went for his plan, he was in for some real trouble. Already Emily had him wrapped so tightly around her little finger, he felt guilty for not sitting down right there in the middle of the corridor and playing action figures. "Here. You take my guy and get started. I'll join you as soon as I talk to your mommy."

She eyed the red Ranger, then took the toy from his hand. "Okay."

Jace had no more than set her on the ground and she was talking in a falsetto voice, bobbing the pink Ranger with each word.

Jace let out a sigh. Emily seemed to have dealt with her traumatic run-in with Barstow faster than any of them. He only could hope that eventually he and Shanna could catch up.

He walked to where Shanna watched him from the wheelchair. He knelt down beside her. "Hey."

She smiled. "Hey."

He combed his gaze over her bruised face, her bandaged ribs and finally looked down at the chair.

"I don't need a wheelchair. They just insisted I use it until I'm outside the hospital doors."

He let out a relieved breath. Shanna had been pretty battered by Barstow. At least she hadn't received permanent damage.

"Your hair is growing out. I'm glad."

He tilted his hat back and ran his fingers over the stubble. "You don't like this look? I'm kind of fond of it."

She laughed deep in her throat. A beautiful sound. Her smile faded. "I heard from Linda."

He raised his brows. "She's in jail, right?"

"Yeah."

"What did she say?"

"She apologized."

He didn't know how Linda could ever be sorry enough for all she'd done. He supposed she'd have to reconcile that with her own conscience. She'd have plenty of time to do it while she was behind bars. "You heard what happened with Gable?" Shanna had been questioned ad nauseam while in the hospital, as had he during the past days. But sometimes the police were better at finding out information than providing it.

"You mean, his confession? It was all over the news."

"Of course. Cable news. I'll bet it was a big story." He couldn't help but smile. Amazing that justice had prevailed, despite the power of money. At least it had for Barstow, Gable and Linda. And even for Shanna and him this time. But the people of Palmer weren't faring so well. "Talbot is going into bankruptcy."

A cloud moved over Shanna's face. "I heard. So many people have lost everything."

Jace nodded. He happened to know that Shanna had lost everything, as well. At least financially speaking. She'd been able to save what mattered most. "I have an idea I want to run by you."

She gave him a smile. "What?"

The jittery feeling seized him again, running from sternum to belt buckle. "I'm thinking of expanding my ranch."

"Really?"

He nodded. "I'd like to buy Roger's land and take over his outfitter operation. Dude ranch, trail rides and hiking in the summer. Maybe a little hunting in the fall, too."

"That's a great idea, Jace."

"There's only one problem."

"What's that?"

"I'm not very good with numbers. I think I need an accountant to make the business work."

"You want a recommendation?"

He smiled. It probably hadn't occurred to her that she was out of a job. Maybe she hadn't thought that far ahead. Maybe she was still trying to catch up to everything that had happened. "No, I know just who I want."

She let out a sigh. "Jace…"

"Shanna, I know we haven't known each other long. And maybe you can't forgive me for giving you those sleeping pills and taking that key, but I love you. With everything I have, I do. And I'd really like to see if we can build something together."

She watched him for a moment, then a smile curved over

her lips and spread to her twinkling eyes. "Will you forgive me for selling you out?"

He chuckled. "You mean, for directing Gable to the cabin next door? For giving me a chance to jump him?"

"I'd intended to give you a chance to escape. I should have known that wouldn't be your choice."

He cupped her hands in his. Her skin felt so soft, her bones so delicate. Yet he knew how strong she was. And everything he knew made him want her more. "What do you say? Will you come home with me? Will you let me take care of you and Emily? Help you get back on your feet?"

She looked down at their hands and threaded her fingers with his. When she raised her gaze back to his face, tears sparkled in her eyes. "I love you, too, Jace."

He leaned down and kissed her. Tender. Sweet. Full of love and promise and trust. "I don't want to pressure you. But I cleared out my office. Set it up as a bedroom for you and Emily. You can stay until you feel better, until you get your feet back under you, until you figure out what you want to do."

Shanna laughed again, the sound soft and strong and happy. This time the smile on her lips didn't fade. "I know what I want, Jace. And I can't think of a place Em or I would rather be than with you."

\* \* \* \* \*

*Enjoy a sneak preview of*
*MATCHMAKING WITH A MISSION*
*by B.J. Daniels,*
*part of the* WHITEHORSE, MONTANA *miniseries.*
*Available from Harlequin Intrigue*
*in April 2008.*

**Nate Dempsey has returned to Whitehorse to uncover the truth about his past…**

Nate sensed someone watching the house and looked out in surprise to see a woman astride a paint horse just on the other side of the fence. He quickly stepped back from the filthy second-floor window, although he doubted she could have seen him. Only a little of the June sun pierced the dirty glass to glow on the dust-coated floor at his feet as he waited a few heartbeats before he looked out again.

The place was so isolated he hadn't expected to see another soul. Like the front yard, the dirt road was waist-high with weeds. When he'd broken the lock on the back door, he'd had to kick aside a pile of rotten leaves that had blown in from last fall.

As he sneaked a look, he saw that she was still there, staring at the house in a way that unnerved him. He shielded his eyes from the glare of the sun off the dirty window and studied her, taking in her head of long blond hair that feathered out in the breeze from under her Western straw hat.

She wore a tan canvas jacket, jeans and boots. But it was

the way she sat astride the brown-and-white horse that nudged the memory.

He felt a chill as he realized he'd seen her before. In that very spot. She'd been just a kid then. A kid on a pretty paint horse. Not this one—the markings were different. Anyway, it couldn't have been the same horse, considering the last time he had seen her was more than twenty years ago. That horse would be dead by now.

His mind argued it probably wasn't even the same girl. But he knew better. It was the way she sat the horse, so at home in a saddle and secure in her world on the other side of that fence.

To the boy he'd been, she and her horse had represented freedom, a freedom he'd known he would never have—even after he escaped this house.

Nate saw her shift in the saddle, and for a moment he feared she planned to dismount and come toward the house. With Ellis Harper in his grave, there would be little to keep her away.

To his relief, she reined her horse around and rode back the way she'd come.

As he watched her ride away, he thought about the way she'd stared at the house—today and years ago. While the smartest thing she could do was to stay clear of this house, he had a feeling she'd be back.

Finding out her name should prove easy, since he figured she must live close by. As for her interest in Harper House… He would just have to make sure it didn't become a problem.

* * * * *

*Be sure to look for*
*MATCHMAKING WITH A MISSION*
*and other suspenseful Harlequin Intrigue stories,*
*available in April*
*wherever books are sold.*

# the DEVIL'S footprints

## Don't miss the latest thriller from

# AMANDA STEVENS

## On sale March 2008!

# SAVE $1.00

## off the purchase price of THE DEVIL'S FOOTPRINTS by Amanda Stevens.

Offer valid from March 1, 2008 to May 31, 2008. Redeemable at participating retail outlets. Limit one coupon per purchase.

52608155

5 65373 00076 2   (8100) 0 11460

MAS2530CPN

# REQUEST YOUR FREE BOOKS!

## 2 FREE NOVELS PLUS 2 FREE GIFTS!

HARLEQUIN®

# INTRIGUE®

## Breathtaking Romantic Suspense

# HARLEQUIN Romance

## presents

*The Wedding Planners*

### *Planning perfect weddings...*
### *finding happy endings!*

Amidst the rustle of satins and silks, the scent of red roses and white lilies and the excited chatter of brides-to-be, six friends from Boston are The Wedding Belles—they make other people's wedding dreams come true....

But are they always the wedding planner...never the bride?

Who will be the next to say "I do"?

**In April:** Shirley Jump, *Sweetheart Lost and Found*
**In May:** Myrna Mackenzie, *The Heir's Convenient Wife*
**In June:** Melissa McClone, *S.O.S. Marry Me*
**In July:** Linda Goodnight, *Winning the Single Mom's Heart*
**In August:** Susan Meier, *Millionaire Dad, Nanny Needed!*
**In September:** Melissa James, *The Bridegroom's Secret*

*And don't miss the exciting wedding-planner tips and author reminiscences that accompany each book!*

www.eHarlequin.com                    HR17507

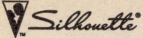

## Silhouette®

## Romantic
# SUSPENSE

### Sparked by Danger, Fueled by Passion.

### *The Taken*

Tierney Doyle is used to being criticized for
her psychic abilities, yet the tough-as-nails—
and drop-dead-gorgeous—detective has no doubt
about what she has uncovered in the case of a
string of unsolved murders. And Tierney is slowly
discovering that working so close to her partner,
detective Wade Callahan, could be lethal.

## Look for

# *Danger Signals*
# by Kathleen Creighton

*Available in April wherever books are sold.*

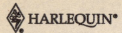 **HARLEQUIN®**

# INTRIGUE®
## COMING NEXT MONTH

### #1053 MATCHMAKING WITH A MISSION by B.J. Daniels
*Whitehorse, Montana*
No matter how much Nate Dempsey's past haunted him,
McKenna Bailey couldn't keep him off her mind. He'd returned to town
to bury his troubled youth—but she wouldn't stop pursuing him until
he was working the ranch by her side.

### #1054 POSITIVE I.D. by Kathleen Long
*The Body Hunters*
In order to save his family from ruthless killers, Will Connor made the
ultimate sacrifice. Dying. Now facing the greatest challenge of his life,
Will must come out of hiding to rescue his captive wife, Maggie, and
protect his family when they need him the most.

### #1055 72 HOURS by Dana Marton
*Thriller*
Parker McCall never stopped loving Kate Hamilton. So when rebels
attack the Russian embassy and take his ex-wife hostage, Parker gets
to prove it. Unsanctioned and nearly impossible, this mission's nothing
without showing Kate the man—the secret agent—he really is.

### #1056 SILENT WITNESS by Leona Karr
With a killer hunting for the witness to his terrible crime, an entire
town was at stake. Detective Ryan Darnell had more than one life
to save—yet teacher Marian Richards may be the most valuable of
them all.

### #1057 I'LL BE WATCHING YOU by Tracy Montoya
Adriana Torres was headed for heartbreak, and Detective Daniel Cardenas
was the last person she needed on her protection detail. Worse, Daniel
wouldn't let Adriana out of his sight—but neither would a killer who
everyone thought was dead.

### #1058 LOVING THE ENEMY by Pat White
Kyle McKendrick vowed to protect Andrea Franks at all costs from the
rogue military faction hunting her. But Kyle was a mercenary, and the one
man she could never forgive. Even if everything she knew about him was
wrong.

www.eHarlequin.com

HICNM0308